WITH THE MAGIC

DONNA K. WEAVER

1

1850

GARETH HILDEBRAND, EIGHTH EARL OF Kellworth, burst into Twickenham Manor, his mind abuzz with his new realization and fear that he had arrived too late.

"Where is Aunt Nellie?" he demanded of the poor servant who was carrying a tray of drinks for guests at the Full Moon Ball.

"Third floor, my Lord," the little woman squeaked.

Gareth took the stairs by twos, not resting until he'd reached the third floor. A light came from down that hall. He ran to it and thrust open the door.

The Americans were gathered there as he'd suspected, standing in front of a large portrait of the five of them. Silver-haired "Aunt" Nellie hurried over to him.

"I'm sorry, my Lord, but this is a private party."

Gareth raised a hand, and she snapped her mouth closed. He looked at Clarisse Hamilton, the rebel, the crusader. Her kindness and feisty spirit had opened his heart to the possibility of love again. She'd shown him a different way to view his world.

"You leave now, from here," he said, forcing back any emotion in his voice.

"My lord," Nellie said, her hands fluttering.

"I asked my physician about the blood incompatibilities you mentioned. He's never heard of such a thing and said anyone suggesting them must be mad. Yet you spoke of them with such confidence," he said. "I know you are not insane, so where you come from such advanced information must be widely known. The only explanation is that you are from another time and not simply another place."

Nellie gave a soft moan.

"From decades in the future," Clarisse said, her expression soft, full of sympathy and understanding.

Gareth felt an initial surge of triumph; he'd been correct. But he wanted her love, not her pity.

"My dears," Aunt Nellie said, glancing nervously at a large hourglass sitting on a table, "We must do this soon, or you will stay another month."

"Everyone get in position," Clarisse said, taking control of the situation, as she always had. "I'll be right there."

"Sorry, but I'm not risking only one of us going back home." Jem Taylor, the interloper, the commoner who'd won Clarisse's heart, laced their fingers.

Gareth wanted to step between them, to pull their hands apart. But he could not; he'd given his word.

Clarisse towed both men to a corner of the room.

"Are you okay?" she asked Gareth.

So many things flashed through his mind. How could he make her understand that he'd been like one dead, merely going through the motions of a life, how she had wakened him to a world of possibilities, opened his heart to loving again? As before, he could not.

Gareth darted a glance at Jem. "I will be if I know he will make you happy."

"I will, my Lord." The man had the nerve to bring their clasped hands to his chest as though to rub his success in Gareth's face. "I make you the same promise I made her." Jem Taylor said the words with all sincerity, and the love in his eyes as he looked at Clarisse gave a little peace to Gareth's heart.

"Am I dead in your time?" he asked.

"Yes," Clarisse said, her voice soft.

"Then be sure, young man," Gareth pointed a finger in the American man's face, "that if you do not make her happy, I will *haunt* you."

"What will you do now, Gareth?" Clarisse asked.

What would he have done if his sister had not met Clarisse here at Twickenham and befriended her? If she had not come to Kellworth for a visit and bullied him into being a better man? So often he'd wanted to hear her say his given name. Only now, when she was betrothed to another man, did she grant his request. Staring at her lovely face, he was glad to see her sincere regard for him. At least he had not lost that.

"My sister and I will continue what you have begun," he said. "I've found more purpose in the last fortnight than I've had my entire life."

"You and your sister have the power to save the lives of generations to come." Jem shot an odd glance at Aunt Nellie.

"Into position," she said with a smile.

"Thank you," Gareth said.

"Thank *you*." Clarisse stood on tiptoe and kissed his cheek.

Gareth was so tempted to steal a kiss, and he gave Jem Taylor a wicked grin, hoping for a response. The man complied, his entire body stiffening. Smirking, Gareth bowed and stepped back to the door where he hesitated, not sure he wanted to leave.

"Make haste!" Nellie glanced at the hourglass again. "Stand before yourself in the portrait and be sure to touch it."

When Clarisse stepped into Jem's arms, Gareth could stand it no longer. He left the room, fully intending to depart, but he stopped at the top of the stairs. What was he to do now? His future was behind him in that room.

This evening, possibly for the first time in his life, he was taking a selfless action. He was allowing her to walk away. What rational woman would choose a common man over an earl?

Clarisse, of course. *Reese.*

Strains of music from the Twickenham Full Moon Ball drifted up to him. How could those people dance gaily while Gareth stood here like a lost soul?

He forced himself to stride down the stairs. At the bottom, he peered at the entrance to the ballroom. For once, his sister had chosen not to attend the monthly ball, blue-deviled that her new friend Clarisse was returning to America. He sympathized with her sentiment.

Outside, a Twickenham groom recognized the earl and brought Gareth his horse. He mounted and glanced back at the manor, still alight for the ball. He may have reasoned that people from the future were able to travel here, but he didn't understand how it was possible. And his instincts told him that Reese and the other Americans could not have been the first.

Gareth had a memory for dates, something his secretary appreciated, not being required to remind him of appointments, especially during Parliament. Gareth searched it now, sure the Americans had arrived at the last Twickenham Ball. He gave himself a mental chide. It mattered not. Reese had made her choice, and he mustn't dwell on this any longer.

He glanced at the full moon, grateful for it and a clear sky to light his way home. As he did, something niggled at the back of his mind, and he shifted his gaze back to the house. Did Aunt Nellie hold her balls on the full moon each month to cover the arrival of travelers in time?

Was it a coincidence that Aunt Nellie's American guests had arrived on the night of a full moon and now had departed during one? Or was this evidence that Aunt Nellie had a reason for holding her monthly balls then? Two such facts might be merely an interesting accident. He must speak with his sister about it. Ellen might be nearly fifteen years his junior, but he'd lately discovered her to be much more intelligent than he'd given her credit for. Thanks to Reese.

With a grunt, he urged his horse forward. What other goings-on had been occurring at Twickenham Manor that Aunt Nellie might wish to cover with her balls? Looking back, he recalled that she often had, as guests, American ladies visiting England in search of husbands with titles. She also hosted the occasional American man seeking a wife. Usually Ellen spoke of individual guests. Had he met other travelers of time?

How many had there been over the years? Had any of them found love in this time and stayed?

As Gareth rode, he allowed his thoughts to drift to Reese again. He gave a dark chuckle. It had been her use of words like "lightyears" and worry about a blood incompatibility between parents and a newborn that could cause the babe to sicken and die that had sent his mind ablaze. Her knowledge of the symptoms and the cause had been too forceful to have been a flight of fancy.

Earlier in the evening, thinking of her, her offhand comments had struck him. He'd considered the impossible—that Reese was not from this time. What a marvelous future where physicians had the knowledge to cure illnesses that people of his time knew nothing about.

At the Kellworth stable, Gareth turned his horse over to a sleepy groom and strode toward his home. He paused to scan the grand manor. How could Reese not have wanted to be mistress of all of this? He would have given her anything she wanted, would have aided her in whatever crusades to do good that she wished.

Yet he, with his title and his lands, had not been enough for her. Never before had a woman he desired not reciprocated. When he had met and fallen in love with Cecily, she'd welcomed his attentions. It had not been difficult to capture her love. That a Hildebrand could have been found lacking was an alien idea.

Reese had been so different, unswayed by his wealth, lands,

and social status. Was it that which had appealed to him? Sadly, she'd already given her heart to another man.

Gareth entered the house. His man was waiting for him.

"My Lord, you do not bring her back with you," Ambrose said, his tone disapproving, though Gareth didn't know if it was toward him for being unsuccessful or her in refusing him.

"No." He let him remove his cloak. "She is gone."

"As you say. Lady Ellen will be lonely." Ambrose accepted Gareth's hat. "I will be up presently to help you dress for bed."

"No. You can go to sleep. I have some thinking to do. I could be up late and will see after myself."

"As you wish, my Lord."

The library was a little chilly, in spite of the warm summer evening. Gareth poured himself a drink and went to the window to gaze out on the grounds. For the second time in his life, he was faced with something he couldn't control.

The first time had been when Cecily had died giving birth to their son, who had shortly followed her to the grave. Gareth had felt so helpless. Neither his social status as a peer nor his wealth could give him what he wanted—neither then nor now. He swallowed the lump in his throat. For the first time, grief did not consume him. Another gift from Reese: the ability to move on at last.

His thoughts drifted back to when he'd burst into that room at Twickenham. Aunt Nellie had looked about to *do* something. *She* must be the key to the traveling. Gareth gave a soft grunt. Somehow, that charming and sometimes daft-acting woman knew how to help people travel to a different time.

The eccentric woman had lived there as long as he could remember, with guests always coming and going. His father had commented once that the Miltons had owned the property for generations, ownership always falling on a female of the line.

Gareth thought again of the strange things Reese had said while they'd worked on improvements to his tenant village.

She'd been almost obsessed with infection and insisted on cleaning, speaking of odd things like "germ theory." Claiming to have had some training in the medical profession, she'd known a great deal and acted as though her knowledge was commonplace.

What discoveries had they made in the future? Was the world she lived in a paradise where everyone knew such information? Was it a place where they had done away with disease? Would Cecily and his son have lived had they been born in that place? A desire to see the wonders of her time filled him.

Gareth sat in his favorite chair, staring at the bookshelves. There was so much knowledge there, but he had rarely availed himself of it. Could *he* travel to the future?

Aunt Nellie was the key, and Gareth Hildebrand was determined to convince her to unlock the door for him.

Present Day

CATHERINE RYAN WATCHED as the group of five Americans descended the stairs of the broad staircase at Twickenham Manor. She'd danced with the tall man, and he'd been quite pleasant. He'd mentioned his regret at only being able to join his friends in time for the ball. It marked the end of Aunt Nellie's weeklong Regency immersive vacation.

Curious, Catherine noted how attentive he now was to the tall woman he had his arm around. Earlier, it'd been entertaining to watch the two of them interact. The space around them had practically crackled with their attraction, yet they'd seemed to circle each other as though opponents in a fencing match.

Now, his manner toward her showed a higher level of intimacy, much more than had been present earlier. However, the woman also showed signs of having been crying. What could have happened to bring them together so quickly? There was obviously a story; there always seemed to be stories here.

That was what continued to draw Catherine back to Twickenham each month. She'd always been a people watcher, and she enjoyed the assortment of personalities she found here. Over the last year, she'd attended nearly a dozen of Aunt Nellie's monthly balls, and it was the story potential that had drawn Catherine back. Perhaps she might one day become a writer like her father, but one of fiction. Doctors could be writers too.

She continued to watch the Americans and smiled. Her experiences here would lend themselves well to a romance novel.

Catherine gave a soft chuckle. Two others in the group were now a couple when they hadn't been earlier in the evening. She squinted to see better. Was she imagining it or did they seem more tanned than they had been earlier? Catherine shook her head. She was being fanciful now.

She looked at the stairs they'd just descended, tempted to climb them. One guest at an earlier ball had commented that they weren't allowed on the fourth floor. That had intrigued Catherine. Like an itch she couldn't scratch, she'd wanted to investigate. Her curiosity had always made her good at her job. She liked to look beyond the obvious.

Whenever she'd observed anomalies at Nellie's, they'd always seemed to come from upstairs. Since the first time Catherine had toured the house, she'd felt a pull to seek out whatever was up those stairs. She let out a breath; she should return to the ballroom.

The Americans were passing her, and the tall woman who'd been crying said something that sent a chill down Catherine's spine.

"I can't bear that they're all dead now."

Dead? The comment brought a macabre feel to the evening, and Catherine's curiosity-itch flared. She peered at the stairs again with narrowed eyes; she *had* to investigate.

But, if Aunt Nellie were to discover Catherine up there, would she be banned from coming to Twickenham again? She reminded herself that "curiosity killed the cat." In her mind, her grandmother's voice finished the old adage, "But satisfaction brought him back."

Still, Catherine needed to ask herself if the risk would be worth it. These balls had become the one bright spot in her life. If she were to lose them too . . .

Then the ever-present pull gave a stronger tug, the sense that there was something else going on and she *must* investigate. The American woman had said "they" were dead. Catherine was a doctor. Surely she had a responsibility to investigate.

Glancing to make sure she was alone, she picked up her skirts and began the climb. Winded by the time she reached the last landing before the fourth floor, she paused to catch her breath, vowing to start exercising regularly. Catherine had been blessed with a fast metabolism, so people were forever thinking she was fitter than she was.

She climbed the last flight. The hallway was unremarkable, lined with paintings. Listening for the sounds of movement, she examined the portraits as she went down the hallway. She heard nothing, and she didn't smell blood.

One door stood open, so she let the tug lead her inside. The long room's Gothic décor was typical of the rest of the house but held nothing but more paintings. How odd. There were a few chairs scattered around, but it didn't look like it was meant to be a regular gathering place for people to sit together and talk.

Most of the pictures were busts of individuals, but in the center of the room hung a large painting of five people, three women and two men. Catherine blinked. It was the Americans, and their painted images wore the same clothing the five had on tonight. She shivered.

The young man she'd danced with hadn't attended the Regency immersion vacation, having only arrived that day. When had someone had time to paint him? She'd also never heard that Twickenham had an artist on staff.

She studied the rest of the pictures in the room. Some were dressed in Regency clothing, but there were many others that spanned several eras. The one with the Americans was the only picture of such a large group. Whoever had arranged the paintings lacked any sense of design, leaving large sections of the walls empty.

That pull came again, as though Catherine had a string attached to her chest that drew her. This time it was to a portrait of a man placed to the right of the one with the Americans. Catherine came to stand before his painting, wondering who he was.

He appeared to be a little older than she was with a few silver strands at his temples. He also had what she'd call a regal bearing. She worked with enough surgeons and specialists who were used to being in charge, and this man had that look about him. He also wore an expression of someone with a fierce determination, the type of man people would steer clear of.

Catherine stepped closer to the painting. Behind the force of will that he projected, he had pain etched on his face. Her heart ached for him. What had happened to mark him that way?

At the sound of rustling skirts, she spun around. Aunt Nellie stood in the doorway, watching her. Catherine's heart leapt into her throat. Would she be kicked out?

The silver-haired woman watched her for a second with an assessing gaze, but there was also a twinkle in it.

"Dr. Ryan, may I help you with something?"

"I overheard—" Catherine broke off.

The American's words sounded ridiculous now. She couldn't very well suggest people had been killed and were hidden on Aunt Nellie's forbidden floor. There was obviously another explanation, and Catherine had played the fool. She took a deep breath.

"I apologize for presuming to come here uninvited. I'm interested in these paintings." She pointed to the large one of the group. "I find it especially curious that I just saw these people come downstairs a few minutes ago."

Aunt Nellie seemed to study the picture before she finally walked to it.

"On occasion, we're able to paint some of our guests. This particular party was most unusual, but I believe it came out quite well." With the corner of her mouth twitching, she gave Catherine a sidelong glance.

Wearing that sly look, Aunt Nellie proved that she knew something but had no intention of sharing it. Curious.

"They all have a similar style to them," Catherine said. "They're quite lovely. Who's the painter?"

"Why, I am."

"You?" Catherine's gaze darted back to the determined man's portrait before she looked at Nellie and said, "I didn't know you painted."

"One learns many skills over the years."

The older woman stepped to the small portrait of the man and ran a finger down the frame. She glanced from it to Catherine and back again. The scrutiny was discomforting but, at least, it didn't appear that she'd be thrown out of the manor.

"Well, I suppose I should leave. I appreciate that you allowed me to see this." Catherine had taken a step toward the door but that strange pull tugged at her again. She paused. "Maybe I could commission you to do a painting of me."

"Yes," Aunt Nellie said with one of her charming, delighted smiles, an odd assessing gleam in her eyes. She glanced at the picture of the man again. "I think I would like very much to paint you."

2

1850

GARETH ROSE EARLY THE NEXT morning, surprising his man.

"'Tis barely nine, my Lord." Ambrose looked a little peeved to have his routine disrupted. "As you were up quite late last night, I didn't expect to see you before Noon."

"I am a man with a mission." Gareth's thoughts had kept him up most of the night, too busy for something as trivial as sleep. He indicated his dressing room. "I make for Twickenham as soon as you've dressed me. Make haste, man."

"Will you not break your fast before you depart, my Lord?"

"Did you not hear me?"

"You are a man with a mission, my Lord." Ambrose heaved out an aggrieved breath and walked into the closet.

Gareth's entire staff seemed surprised to find him up so early, which irritated him. Had he not risen early for nearly a fortnight to assist Reese with her work on his tenant village? Though she had come only once after she'd accepted Taylor's offer of marriage, Gareth had returned many times to assess the progress and check in on his cottiers. He had desired to prove to her that he would, indeed, carry on her work when she returned to America.

In his haste, he found himself sharper with the staff than he should have been and took a moment to calm himself. He'd learned in the House of Lords that he must have a cool head during negotiations, and he did not doubt for one minute that it would take a great deal to convince Aunt Nellie. He must not risk putting her off. He wanted—no, *needed*—her to help him travel to the future.

"Please order my horse, Ambrose."

"I already have, my Lord." His valet lifted Gareth's riding cloak.

"Good man." Gareth let him settle it on his shoulders. With his gloves and hat, he strode from his room.

He spent the ride to Twickenham reviewing his argument. Upon arrival, he found Aunt Nellie standing at the manor's entrance, waiting for him. It did not come as a surprise. She also didn't look particularly pleased to see him.

Considering how he'd burst into that room last night, he should have expected it. A part of him wished he'd remained to see Nellie send her American guests off to the future.

Gareth dismounted and handed his reins to a waiting groom. He strode up the stairs, bowed, and took Aunt Nellie's hand.

"What brings you here so early, my Lord?" While her expression wasn't welcoming, neither was it stiff. Did that mean she would aid him or attempt to keep him from what he wanted?

"I wish to speak with you about what happened last night." At his words, Aunt Nellie's expression took on a hard edge.

"You must understand, my Lord, that I will not allow you to go to the future in an attempt to stop them from marrying."

"I meant what I said to her, that I wish them happy. What I desire is to see this future."

Aunt Nellie arched a brow. In the contrary way he'd had as a child with his tutor, a sense of pleasure filled Gareth that he had surprised her. She considered him for a few seconds, her head tilted, almost as though she were listening to someone who whispered in her ear. A myriad of emotions seemed to flash across her face, the most prominent one humor. It made him wary, and his pleasure disappeared.

"Perhaps you should come to my office, my Lord."

He offered Aunt Nellie his arm, and she took it. They didn't speak until she'd closed the door and invited him to take a seat. She sat at her desk with her elbows on the arms of her chair, her fingers steepled as she studied him.

"This is a rather unique situation, my Lord," she finally said, her tone disapproving. "Most often, it is an accident that brings guests from other times. It is not my role here for Twickenham to become a way-station for people wishing to gad about."

A flicker of something in her expression gave the lie to her words, and a wave of hope filled him.

"I have not before had someone who was not already an unexpected traveler request this of me. I must say I'm disappointed that Clarisse was indiscreet enough that you deduced where she was from. I have no wish to be burned at the stake as a witch."

"Blood and thunder, woman," Gareth exclaimed, incredulous. "Pardon my language, but they haven't done that in nearly a century and a half. It's stuff and nonsense anyway."

"Says the man who wishes me to transport him to the future," Aunt Nellie said dryly.

Gareth stared at her for a second and then burst out laughing. "True," he said when he could get his breath. "But do not blame Reese. You know how inquisitive I can be."

"Having been acquainted with you since you were but a lad, I *do* know, my Lord. You have a reputation in the House of Lords for it as well. And your peers have also been known to call you hardheaded."

"Not to my face, they haven't," Gareth said, his tone dangerous. "I have been given a glimpse of something I'm determined to see for myself."

"The future." Aunt Nellie's tone had turned flat. "It is a temptation to see beyond one's lifetime, my Lord. For some it can be disturbing and destructive. It steals their peace of mind."

"I promise that my intent is pure." Gareth leaned forward. "I feel alive for the first time in years."

"Yes, I've seen that Clarisse was able to waken in you the man I knew when you were young." Aunt Nellie clasped her hands, once again studying him. "Were I to share certain information with you, you must understand that I *will* protect it. Have you spoken of this to your sister?"

"I have not." He was glad Ellen had already retired when he'd returned home last night, and he hadn't seen her that morning. Otherwise he might have spoken to her about last night's events, and he sensed that would have been a disaster in Aunt Nellie's eyes.

"You can*not*. Should I hear that you have been indiscreet, I will remove your memory of it."

Gareth blinked. "You're able to do that?"

"Yes, I am." Aunt Nellie unclasped her hands, all the lightheartedness gone from her expression. "*Any* lapse on your part will result in a loss of your memory of it *all*, including Clarisse."

Gareth felt a little sick. She'd changed his life. He *couldn't* lose that. To do so would risk returning to the man he'd been before.

"On my honor, by all I hold dear, I promise I'll not speak of this to anyone, not even my sister."

"Perfect." Aunt Nellie smiled, the mischievous twinkle back in her eyes. She flicked her fingers and a sparkly dust-like substance settled over him, tingling where it touched his bare skin. "You are now bound to your word. Should your lips prove unable to keep your honor, your memory of all that has transpired here will disappear."

Gareth stared at his hands, the muscles twitching. He didn't know how it could be, but something now resided on him—*in* him—and it confirmed that she spoke the truth.

"I will explain things to you, but I wish you to drink some tea before I begin." She rose and rang for a servant, who immediately entered the room carrying a tray. The tiny woman set it on the desk. "Thank you, Lulu."

Gareth recognized her as the Twickenham maid who'd accompanied Reese on her stay at his home.

"Why must I drink tea first?" he asked when the young woman had departed.

"It will help to soothe your nerves."

He shot her a flat look, but she merely smiled.

"Trust me, my Lord. What I share will seem impossible to you."

"More impossible than traveling through time?"

"Trust me." She handed him a cup.

Gareth accepted it and took a hesitant sniff. It had a fragrant bouquet and must be an unusual mix. He took a drink and warmth flowed with it into his stomach, then radiated to the rest of his body. As he finished it, the tension that had consumed him since he'd first pieced together the puzzle of Reese's confusing remarks eased. He felt . . . *mellow*.

He wanted to laugh. Gareth Hildebrand, mellow? He doubted he'd ever felt that way in his life. He glanced at his hostess, and she wore one of her knowing smiles.

"I believe I'm sufficiently prepared," he said. "If you soothe me further, I fear I will fall asleep."

"Very well, my Lord." Nellie clasped her hands before her again. "I am a faerie."

Gareth blinked and stared at her, trying to make sense of what she'd said. He'd considered some mechanical device as a means of traveling through time and even an angel but not *this*. Did she dare to mock him? The heat of anger suffused his body, but then it seemed to dampen.

"After all that we've spoken of, you're now giving me a Canterbury tale?" he finally asked with disgust.

"If you cannot trust me in this," she said, leaning back, "there's no point in going any further."

"You're *not* jesting me?" Gareth rubbed his temple.

"No."

She said that single word and nothing more. Gareth could read in her expression that what he said next could end the discussion—and any hope to see the future. If he'd been willing to consider divine intervention in the form of an angel, then why not believe faeries could provide the mode of transportation?

"You're able to conjure with magic?" he asked. "Faerie magic?"

"*Fae* magic, yes, my Lord." Aunt Nellie made a face. "I'm not a witch; I do not *conjure*."

"How does it work?"

"My Lord, perhaps you would be more interested in *why* we fae are here and not living with our own kind."

"Yes, I believe I would." Gareth nodded. "Please, proceed."

"I'm a guardian for ancient fae ley lines," Nellie said. "There are small releases of magic daily that don't affect people. However, at the full moon there's a much more powerful discharge. Anciently, an early version of Twickenham Manor was constructed over the lines as a protection against these periodic releases of magic. Should people be in the right place when this happens, they are moved through time."

Gareth frowned, feeling more than a little dismayed. If the travel through time was accidental, how was he to make his own journey?

"Are you telling me that it was mere happenstance that Reese and her friends returned home?"

"No, it was happenstance that they first traveled to this time. I understand what you are truly asking—if their return to the future was planned."

"Yes. I want to know if they could have traveled here originally by design."

"Magic causes the traveling. One may return to a specific time only if there is something to anchor them." At his confused look,

Aunt Nellie added, "It does not matter if you understand. What's of importance is that you trust what I say. One does not need to understand the mechanics of a steam engine in order to avail oneself of a train's ability to move from one location to another."

"True enough." He pondered her words, tapping his fingers on the arm of his chair. "What is the anchor?"

"A painting."

Like the one Reese and her companions had been standing in front of when he'd burst in upon them.

"Then, in order for me to travel to the future when the magic next releases," he mused, "there must be a painting for me to travel to?"

"Yes, if you wish to visit a particular point in time." Aunt Nellie gave him a wry smile. "An accidental release of magic could send you to any time period."

Gareth considered that. He didn't wish to make an accidental journey to some other time, especially if he might not be able to return. As much as he wished to see this future that Reese had come from, he had responsibilities to his sister. He had no heir, and the only male relative in line to inherit was an inept wastrel. Gareth could not trust his sister's future in the hands of such a man.

As he contemplated making the journey to the future, he thought of Grandmama's wish that he remarry. His great aunt's demand that he get an heir soon carried more weight than it had before. Too much rested upon Gareth remaining alive and hearty, so he could father an heir and train him in his duties. The Kellworth lands and tenants had suffered enough because Gareth had left the responsibility of their care in the hands of an incompetent steward.

"If you were to paint my portrait in this time, would it then serve as an anchor in a future time?"

Aunt Nellie gave the hint of a smile and nodded. "I could place you anywhere along the time line that has your picture."

"Because of a painting."

"They're very special paintings."

"Magical?"

Aunt Nellie simply smiled at him. Of course it was magical.

"If I were to appear in a future Twickenham Manor, what would they think?"

"I'm a faerie, my Lord." Her voice held a hint of smugness. "I would be there to greet you."

Gareth gave a little gasp. Was she saying she was an immortal being or merely a very long-lived one? Not that it mattered.

"Will you remember me?"

"Of course."

"When must I return here?"

"The magic is telling me it is important for you to make this journey. You may stay as long as you wish, but you are only able to travel during a full moon." Aunt Nellie raised a finger. "You could return to nearly the exact time you left, so it appeared as though you'd been gone for the blink of an eye." She held up another finger. "You may also return to some other full moon."

"But only on a full moon." Gareth nodded, gratified that he'd been correct on that issue as well. "I would wish to return the same night I left. How long will it take for you to paint my portrait?"

"Since I didn't receive any accidental travelers this month, I should be able to do a simple portrait by the next full moon."

"I must wait so long?"

"Yes, my Lord," Aunt Nellie said, her voice placid. But her eyes danced as they did when she knew something that others did not. It made the hair stand up on the back of his neck. She asked, "Will that suit?"

It appeared it must if he were to make this journey.

"It will, and I thank you."

"Don't forget your promise, my Lord."

"Even in the future?"

"Our position is precarious, even then. The ley lines *must* be protected."

"And people protected from the ley lines."

"Exactly so. The fissure that releases the magic continues to grow, making it necessary to add on to the manor. If you visit the future, you'll find a larger structure, likely with an additional floor or two."

His curiosity was piqued even further with this information, but he said no more about it.

"What clothing should I bring?" he asked. "I must dress according to the fashions of the day."

"Come dressed as you wish. Our monthly balls are always held on the full moon to help account for the arrival of any accidental guests we may receive. My future-self will be able to see to your needs."

Gareth nodded, fighting disappointment at the long wait.

"Have you broken your fast yet, my Lord?"

His stomach chose that moment to growl. "I have not."

"I invite you to dine with me then." She rose, and Gareth stood as well.

"It would be a pleasure," he said, following her to the office door. "How many members of your staff know of this?"

"All of my staff are also fae," she said.

He tried to hide his surprise, but it must have shown because she gave him her now-familiar knowing smile.

"What of your nephew?" Gareth knew and liked William Milton and would never have dreamed the man was fae.

"He's my *adopted* nephew, but he knows."

"Ah. I imagine that must be an interesting story."

"Indeed." Aunt Nellie shrugged but said nothing more.

Gareth would have liked to quiz her further but chose not to. His journey meant too much to him to risk it by prying into what was a personal matter.

In four weeks, he would experience a utopia.

3

PRESENT DAY

OVER THE NEXT FEW WEEKS, on the days Catherine didn't work, she went to Twickenham Manor to sit for Aunt Nellie.

"Why not just take my picture and paint from that?" Catherine asked on the third week. She'd questioned the older woman about it earlier, but Aunt Nellie had gone cryptic.

"I thought you were enjoying your visits here." Nellie glanced over the top of her glasses. She wore one of those all-knowing-teacher expressions she used when people asked stupid questions.

"You know I am, but I'm interested in what goes into this creative process of yours." Catherine scanned the portraits in the room where they hung. "I've always been into science and hard facts but not very artistic. Someday I'd love to develop that in myself."

"Then I will answer your question." Aunt Nellie shifted the position of Catherine's face again. "A photograph of a person is dead, and I can create a painting from one. However, I do my best work from living models. I'm able to work on it from memory but often need additional interaction to fix the image again which can shift with the passage of time."

"Interesting." Catherine kept her expression unchanged but let her gaze shift back to the painting of the man again. "Is this a talent that you inherited from your ancestors? Some of these paintings look to be quite old. That one, for example."

"Yes. That was painted in 1850." The corners of Aunt Nellie's mouth twitched like she was trying not to smile, as though she were privy to an inside joke.

Catherine had discovered that her hostess seemed to do that a lot but would never explain when asked about it. Of course, she seemed to see a lot of things as humorous. It was a personality trait that Catherine wished she could emulate. Her late husband's most common complaint had been that she was too serious and didn't take the time to see how funny life was.

She shifted against the ache in her back, glad she didn't have to deal with stays too. Aunt Nellie had insisted that Catherine wear a different kind of dress than the Regency gown she had worn to the balls. The blue dress had beautiful beading and fit her better than any dress she'd ever worn.

"Do you need to take a break?" Aunt Nellie asked. "You can't seem to sit still this evening."

"I'm sorry." Catherine rose and stretched. As she so often did whenever she visited Twickenham now, she went to stand in front of the man's portrait. Ever since she'd first seen it, she hadn't been able to stop thinking about him. He'd even invaded her dreams on a few occasions. "If you know what year this one was painted, do you know anything about him?"

"Yes." Aunt Nellie stepped beside her and straightened the frame unnecessarily. "His name was Gareth Hildebrand, the eighth earl of Kellworth. It was a neighboring estate."

"So many of the great houses were lost with the shift from a rural economy." Catherine pressed her hand against her leg to keep from touching his face as she often did when she came here alone. It would be embarrassing for Nellie to know how obsessed Catherine had become over the painting of a dead man. "I wonder what he thought of all the changes he saw over his lifetime. He could have lived long enough to see the dawn of a new century."

"One must learn to be flexible with change for it is the one constant." Aunt Nellie gave a soft smile. "Shall we begin again?"

"All right." Catherine took her seat and let herself be adjusted and arranged until she was in the right position again. "Why did you decide to have me wear this style?"

"This is best because the gown becomes your figure, and that color of blue goes well with your flaxen locks."

Flaxen locks, Catherine mouthed to herself. No one had ever called her dark blonde curls that before.

As Aunt Nellie went back to painting, Catherine thought about how the comment flattered a romantic side of her personality that she'd been trying to find again over the last year. It was one of the reasons she'd started coming to the balls. As a teen, she'd always felt like an oddball, the science nerd who secretly read her mother's Gothic romances. The intellectually elitist group she'd spent her time with in school had shunned those kinds of books. Because she'd wanted to fit in somewhere, she'd done the same thing.

When she'd first married, she and her husband had been walking by an old bookstore, and she'd seen a novel by Victoria Holt that Catherine had loved as a young teen. She hadn't read for pleasure in years and paused to look at it, thinking how much she'd enjoyed it. Her husband had scoffed at the novel, surprised that she would even look at "rubbish like that." She was twenty-seven after all. Catherine had realized he only saw a part of who she was and reading romances hadn't fit the image she'd chosen. Since she hadn't read a romance in years, and it hadn't been important, she'd walked on.

After she'd lost him, Catherine had spent a lot of time reflecting on her life and the choices she'd made. One way she'd dealt with her grief had been to go in search of her old self. What was wrong with being the left-brained doctor at work and a right-brained romantic on her own time? She'd spent the last eighteen months reading all the old Gothic romances she could get her hands on. Only then had she understood how much of herself she'd buried. She was done with that and had spent the last year rediscovering what she liked.

"I believe one more sitting for some final touches, and I'll have this finished," Aunt Nellie said, pulling Catherine from her ruminations.

"Believe it or not, I'll miss these sessions." Catherine stood and stretched. "I've enjoyed coming here."

"As one of my American guests once told me, you needn't be a stranger. You're always welcome." Aunt Nellie turned the painting toward Catherine.

Unexpected tears made it difficult to see. She blinked rapidly and stepped closer. What more did Nellie need to add to it? It was beautiful as it was. Catherine wished her parents were still alive. It would have made a wonderful gift for her mother.

As always, her gaze drifted to the painting of the man. Gareth. Catherine liked the name. It seemed to fit him. Only then did she notice his portrait was the same size as hers. She tilted her head, looking between the two. It was almost as though the two went together as a set.

"Have you ever considered selling any of these?" she asked.

"I'm sorry, but no." Aunt Nellie wore one of her soft, knowing smiles. "Gareth's is a recent addition."

Catherine frowned. She'd been so captivated by the man in the painting that her normally observant mind hadn't connected the dots. She knew that painting was *old,* but Nellie had also said that *she'd* painted the portraits. Frowning, Catherine scanned the other pictures in the room. They all showed signs of age.

"I thought you said *you* painted these."

"Why, yes, I did."

"Do you use an aging technique?"

"You could say that." There was so much humor in Nellie's

voice that Catherine thought the older woman might giggle but instead she asked, "Will you be attending my ball next week?"

"I'd been planning on it, but I've been asked to take someone's shift." Catherine hadn't missed a ball since she'd started attending them.

"I believe you shouldn't miss this one." There was something intense in the older woman's voice.

"Why?" Catherine asked, suddenly wary.

"It's just a feeling I have." She chuckled, and the delightful sound seemed to take away Catherine's alarm. "We're opening the event to allow full-length ball gowns from any age, even modern."

"Really?" Catherine glanced at her dress.

"I think you should wear that gown, if you don't mind." Aunt Nellie made an adjustment to the way the skirt hung and glanced at the painting. "Yes. Please come and wear this."

Something in the woman's voice made it seem very important that Catherine do just that. It sent a thrill through her, hinting at something special to come. It didn't make sense. Why would it matter if there were a larger variety of gowns at the ball or that she wore this dress rather than one of her other gowns?

It didn't matter. She was determined to live her life now the way she wanted to.

"All right. I'll tell him I can't take his shift."

"Excellent. Do you have any plans for the next month or so, any holiday time coming?"

Catherine rubbed her jaw. Aunt Nellie was all over the map with her topics today.

"Yes, I have a couple of weeks accumulated. I've been trying to decide where best to take my holiday. Why?"

"Because I have a special guest who will arrive in time for the ball, but this is my busiest immersion month of the year." Aunt Nellie looked sincerely frazzled for the first time. "I had hoped to take my visitor around London myself, but it is beyond me at this time. I would like to enlist your aid."

"Mine?" Catherine wondered how she could help and then she groaned. "You want *me* to take him around."

"Yes." Aunt Nellie patted her shoulder. "I'm sure once you meet him you'll understand why. With your schedule as you've explained it to me, you work three very long days but then have four days off. It shouldn't be difficult to take an extra one off each week, should it?"

"Each week? How long will he be here?"

"A month, so it's only four days. That's a good trade for a painting, isn't it?" Nellie gave her most charming smile. "Now, let's get you out of that gown."

"YOU'VE BEEN on edge of late, Gareth," Ellen said as they drove to Twickenham Manor for the Full Moon Ball. His sister rested her hand on his, concern heavy in her expression. "Are you well?"

"Very well, my dear."

He appreciated that she hadn't brought up Reese, which Ellen had done too often during the first week after the Americans had departed. He hadn't needed the reminder. To occupy his mind, Gareth had thrown himself into managing his estate affairs. He'd visited Aunt Nellie's tenant villages to see how she provided for her cottiers. Ellen had come with him on that visit, and they'd discussed what she envisioned for his own tenants.

"I've enjoyed working with you these past weeks," he said, letting her hear the pride in his voice. "I confess that I've underestimated your talents and merely credited you with a little gift for gardening."

"Thank you." His younger sister's eyes glistened, and her cheeks flushed with pleasure.

After his experience with Reese and her influence on Ellen, followed by his own time spent in her company over the past month, Gareth viewed his sister differently. Once he'd begun soliciting her input on decisions facing him, he' thinking to be logical and insightful. It'd started wit village, but he'd taken to asking her opinion on o estate affairs. He'd been impressed enough with her thoughts that he'd involved her in the decision of hiring a new man of business.

She'd invested her efforts in overseeing all of the estate's tenant villages, so Gareth had accompanied her. He'd been relieved to find that none were in as poor a state as the one that Reese had taken under her wing and then castigated him over. And rightly so. He'd been negligent in his responsibilities there.

When two friends from London, also members of the peerage, had chastised him about his new efforts, he'd been angered. They'd declared he was setting the wrong precedent in investing time and money on ne'er-do-wells. Gareth had tried to assure them that he was not a candidate for Bedlam and was merely experimenting on a new business practice. Reese had argued that the output from a happy, healthy, and trained workforce would more than pay for the cost of any improvements. So far, she'd been correct. And that did not take into consideration the element of compassion.

After speaking with Ellen about it, he'd approached others in nearby estates to see how they handled their tenants. The two that he'd visited were people who had looked at their cottiers much as he once had. When he'd made a few casual suggestions, they'd looked at him askance.

The oldest one had been inflexible and had no intention of changing the way he handled his estate. The other one had been a younger man newly come into his inheritance and hoping to increase his revenues. He'd visited the tenant village at Gareth's invitation and been impressed with how industrious the entire community seemed to be. Ellen had been encouraged by his response.

Gareth's experience with Reese and then with Ellen in managing the estate had also changed how he viewed women. Oh, many of them still fit his previous view that they were emotionally fragile creatures, intellectually inferior. Though, if he were to be honest with himself—and if he had learned nothing, he'd learned to do that—many of the men he considered friends were intellectually inferior as well.

When Gareth had traveled to London and posed some of the same questions to the men at his club that he had discussed at length with his sister, he'd been underwhelmed. Gareth recalled when Reese had used that term against him. The memory still hurt, but he gave a weak smile.

He gave his sister's hand a gentle pat. There was so much more to her than he had allowed himself to see. He must be sure that whomever should win her hand was worthy of her.

As they approached it, Twickenham Manor shone like a beacon, lit as it was for the ball. A storm was brewing, and clouds obscured the full moon. He hoped the poor weather would not prevent him from traveling.

"I believe you should stay the night here," Gareth said. "The roads will be bad if those clouds let loose."

"Yes." Ellen straightened her white gloves. "Aunt Nellie sent a message this afternoon to that effect."

"Good." Gareth took a slow breath. He must survive a few hours of dancing and hobnobbing with Aunt Nellie's other guests. Some time spent in the card room would help. She'd instructed him that he must not arrive in the portrait room until a few minutes before midnight, and he must come alone.

Thus began what seemed to him like an eternal evening. Never had he felt so internally anxious while needing to present his usual bored front. Typically, it wasn't a problem because he was often bored at these events. Even though he had a reputation for not being interested in ever marrying again, there were always the hopeful mamas who would insist on thrusting their eligible daughters his way.

"Well, Kellworth," Lord Radnor said as he approached, "I hear you're turning into quite the philanthropist." He shot a smug glance at his two companions.

Gareth recognized the arrogant manner as one he would have used himself a mere two months ago. It drove home more than anything else how much he and his sister had been changed by the accidental visit of an American woman from the future. He didn't bother to share with the man how the Kellworth tenants were no longer broken, that the children played happily as they should, now looking healthy and well fed. He would never be able to explain the feeling of riding into his tenant village to be greeted by his cottiers as a savior of sorts.

Lord Radnor was older, and he wouldn't care. Gareth knew all about subtle persuasion and had found younger men to be more open to suggestions.

"I imagine there are some who would say that." Gareth flicked some imaginary lint from his jacket sleeve. "I am, however, looking to increase the revenues from my estates. Aunt Nellie had some American guests who shared some unique approaches that I thought worth a try. It was time to make some improvements anyway, so it seemed a good time."

"Including that you are investing quite a bit of capital on your tenants?" Lord Radnor peered at him through a quizzing glass.

"It is simple enough. I was recently made aware of the poor condition of my investment." Gareth had memorized the carefully crafted answer after so much negative response during his visit to London. "It's no different from caring for your manor. I know you recently made some major renovations at your seat."

"Ha," the man guffawed. "That was my wife wishing to empty my coffers."

"Even so, if one wishes to have a well-maintained home for entertaining guests, one must make periodic improvements. Our homes can become shabby, as can our other properties. In making these improvements, I've found that my workers are happier and that happier tenants work harder and produce more." Gareth shot each of the men a knowing look. "I expect that I will have recouped my expenses in less than a year, while my tenants will continue to produce at the higher level providing increased estate revenues for years to come."

That created a hearty discussion, and Gareth let the men debate, choosing not to participate himself. Thinking back on it, he felt rather stupid that he hadn't considered some of these things himself.

Gareth glanced at his pocket watch. He needed to make a showing and dance with someone. A quick scan of the room showed it full of mothers with eligible daughters whom he was sure would be thrown his way.

It was something he must consider. He decided he ought to discuss it with Ellen. She might be able to make some suggestions about likely candidates for a new wife, and he would prefer that she and his sister enjoyed each other's company.

An image of Reese filled his mind, and he pushed it aside. He needed a like-minded lady who could be a partner with him on the improvements he desired to make. In his attempts to forget Cecily, he'd pursued light-skirts, none of whom were wife material. He wanted a woman of intelligence and innovation, a woman who was comfortable in society but not afraid to step outside of the mold that society placed upon them all.

To avoid setting tongues wagging, he danced with one of the young ladies who had been deemed a wallflower. He thought Reese would approve.

When he returned, the men were still arguing the merits and disadvantages of investing in their estates. It pleased Gareth that a few of the younger men appeared to be in agreement with his suggestions. He must be patient.

He checked the time again. Everyone would soon be going to the midnight dinner, so it was time for him to make his way upstairs. He'd checked with Ellen to confirm that she had a companion to escort her to the meal.

Gareth quietly slipped out and made his way up the stairs, his pulse quickening in anticipation. The wait had seemed an eternity and reminded him of being a boy and waiting for the arrival of Father Christmas. Aunt Nellie had finished his portrait a fortnight ago. She'd insisted that he must come for several sittings, and he thought it a good likeness.

"Are you ready for this, my Lord?" Aunt Nellie asked, and he turned to face her, his heart racing.

"I am. What would you have me do?"

"First, my Lord," Aunt Nellie said, "I would have you keep an open mind. You will travel well over a hundred and fifty years into the future. Many things will have changed greatly in fashion and in mores. Technology will have advanced in unimaginable ways. The world will have experienced many growing pains. Were you to speak with your great grandfather, he would tell you of a very different time. The society you will visit will be quite different and life will move quickly."

"How do you know this?" he asked with the first feeling of dread. "Have you visited the future?"

"I've had many visitors from the future who have shared this information. From what they've told me, there are amazing inventions that have eased the burden of labors, but they tell me there is also a cost. I cannot say more, as I don't understand it all myself. Just know you must not look like a country bumpkin come to the big city for the first time. If what you see stuns you, you must try not to show it."

"Because I must not look as though I *am* a bumpkin from the past." Gareth put humor in his voice, hoping she wouldn't hear his nervousness. He intended to enjoy this holiday in the future, one way or another. It was he who was making the demand of Aunt Nellie. "I must thank you for granting me this favor."

Her expression turned from serious to mischievous. In all the years he'd known her, he had never realized how often she did that, and he found it irksome.

"You must work *with* the magic, my Lord. I have agreed to this jaunt of yours into the future because the magic tells me you need to do this. I don't know if it is to give you peace of mind, or if there is more to it."

Gareth still found himself of two minds about this magic anyway. He'd accepted that there must be a way to travel to different times because he'd seen the evidence. He must trust that Aunt Nellie wasn't giving him a Banbury story as to the mechanism. As he wished to make this journey, so he would accept whatever conditions Aunt Nellie placed upon him.

"'Tis almost time." She nodded to an hourglass he had noticed when she'd sent off the Americans.

She moved before him and began weaving her hands as she had also done that night a month ago. Aunt Nellie's hands now seemed to glow, and a strange sensation ebbed into him, growing powerful as the brightness increased. The movement of her hands turned frenzied as she molded the light, making him slightly dizzy.

"Off you go, my Lord," she cried.

An uncomfortable tingle ran through his body, turning his stomach. The room blazed as though the sun had come over the horizon, blinding him. He fell back toward the painting.

4

PRESENT DAY

GARETH ROLLED FROM HIS BACK and rose to his knees, his palms on the floor. Closing his eyes, he fought a wave of nausea such as he'd never experienced before. He feared he might lose the contents of his stomach. How humiliating. His heart raced, and he found himself panting. He groaned. If traveling through time made one this ill, he wondered that anyone did it by choice.

"Uh oh," a woman's musical voice said, a touch of humor in her tone. "It looks like someone's overindulged in the punchbowl. Aunt Nellie doesn't allow guests on this floor. How did you make it up here in this condition?"

The sound of rustling skirts was followed by cool, gentle fingers brushing his forehead. She then pressed them against the inside of his wrist. There was something comforting about the sound of her voice, the softness of her touch. It reminded him of what it had been like to have Nurse tend him as a young boy with chickenpox.

"You don't *smell* like you've been drinking. Clammy skin and rapid breaths." The woman's tone changed to concern. "Have you received bad news?"

Gareth tried to shake his head, but the motion made him dizzy. He groaned again.

"I need you to lie down." The woman's surprisingly strong hands pushed him onto his back.

"No," he moaned. "I don't wish to sick up."

"I'll take care of you. Don't worry."

As he fought off the nausea, she lifted his feet and placed something under them. She then started untying his cravat. He grabbed her wrist.

"What are . . . you doing?" Gareth growled, forcing down the pains in his stomach.

"Treating you for shock." With a simple move, she'd freed her hand and was loosening his neck cloth. With his throat free of the binding, his breathing eased, so he didn't protest when she unbuttoned his waistcoat. She then covered him with something. "You need to stay still while I get Aunt Nellie. She'll want to know that one of her guests is ill."

"Aunt Nellie . . . sent me here."

"Up here? Why would—" The woman had started to brush the hair from his forehead and stopped with a little gasp. "That's not possible."

At the disbelief in her voice, Gareth braved opening his eyes and found himself gazing at the face of a beautiful woman. The pale blue of her gown seemed to add sparkles to her striking gray eyes. They weren't those of a girl fresh out of the schoolroom but a woman grown. Life had left its mark in the fine lines on her face. He recognized the pain, for he saw a harsher version every morning when he looked in the mirror.

"Gareth?" she whispered.

He blinked, almost forgetting the discomfort in his stomach. How could this woman know his name? He'd never met her, for he was sure he would never have forgotten her.

"Do I know you?" Gareth asked slowly.

She shook her head and pointed to the wall. He shifted enough to see the painting Nellie had completed of him. The colors were less vibrant now, and the oil showed the cracks of age. Beside it hung another portrait that looked as though it could be a match for his in size and frame, though the paint was recent. He looked back at her.

"You are also a traveler of time?" he asked.

"*What*?" she asked, her brows knitting.

Gareth's mouth went dry, his stomach tightening in a spasm. Perhaps she didn't know about it. Had he triggered Aunt Nellie's spell? Alarmed, he searched his memory and found everything intact. He let out a breath. His muscles relaxed, and the spasms stopped.

"I apologize if I sound befuddled," he said in an attempt to distract her. "I feel disoriented."

"What happened?" The woman pressed the back of her fingers to his forehead again. "Your skin is warmer." She touched them to the base of his throat, which sent his heart racing. "Hmm. Your heartrate is elevated. Have you taken any recreational drugs?"

"I'm in excellent health." Gareth couldn't help feeling a little indignant. "Why would my physician treat me with drugs?"

"You don't seem in excellent health at the moment." Her tone was wry, a smile teasing the corners of her mouth.

"And how would *you* know, miss? Who are *you*?" His question came out sharper than he'd intended.

The woman leaned back. "I'm an A&E doctor. Befuddled is a good description for you. I wonder if you're having a drug reaction. We may need to run a toxicology—"

"Catherine, what's happened?" Aunt Nellie hurried over to them. "Ah, my visitor has arrived. I'm so sorry, my Lord. I had an emergency that took longer than I expected. Bring it in, Lulu."

Gareth stared at Aunt Nellie who was watching him with concern as she waved over a maid carrying a tea tray. She looked just like the Lulu in the past.

"Drink this tea, and you'll feel much better, my Lord." Nellie glanced at the woman who claimed to be a female physician and was getting to her feet. "Catherine, this was not how I'd hoped to introduce you to Lord Hildebrand."

"You mean Gareth Hildebrand, eighth Earl of Kellworth?" the lady doctor asked, her expression disbelieving. "The same one in the portrait that you told me was painted in 1850?"

"Why, yes." The fae woman straightened and matched the physician gaze for gaze. "I suppose I meant to say the portrait was painted in the style fashionable in 1850."

The woman considered him, wary. "All this time I thought you were dead," she finally said.

WATCHING as Aunt Nellie and Lulu helped Gareth to sit up enough to drink the tea, Catherine struggled with a confusion of emotions. How could she be both disappointed and thrilled to see that the man in the painting was here?

She couldn't help feeling like she'd been pranked. The man had been in shock; that had been no act. But why would Nellie have claimed the painting was old and the subject dead when he was very much alive?

None of it made any sense and left Catherine with a bad taste in her mouth, reminding her of when she'd been a young teen and new to England. She'd met many people who got off on pulling pranks, and she'd been the victim too often. What a shame that Aunt Nellie had turned out to be one of them. It was time to go home.

Catherine eased toward the door while the two women were occupied with the man. He'd managed to take a few sips of the tea and was looking much better already. What kind of tea could make such a difference? For how ill he'd looked, his recovery was remarkable.

He stood without help.

"What happened to your neck cloth, my Lord?" Aunt Nellie asked as he went about straightening it.

"*She* happened to it." He shot Catherine an accusing look. "That female claims to be a physician."

"That *female*?" She crossed her arms and sent him her worst glare. "You act as though that's unusual. I'll have you know that nearly half of all doctors in the UK are women. Where have you been hiding, under a rock?"

Gareth looked about to argue with her but then blinked. He glanced at Aunt Nellie, who nodded. He straightened, as though at attention, and gave Catherine a stiff bow.

"My apologies, miss."

"Doctor."

"I am *so* sorry, my Lord," Aunt Nellie said before they could get into it again. "I'd anticipated having the tea for you when you arrived, and you would have been spared the worst of your discomfort."

"You knew I was coming?" he asked.

"For this visit, yes." She shot him a warning glance which made Catherine's hackles rise.

The two of them were obviously part of the prank. Fine. Catherine was well and truly done. She turned and strode from the room.

"Catherine. Wait." Aunt Nellie ran after her. "Where are you going?"

"Home." She paused at the top of the stairs. "Please ship the painting there. I won't be troubling you anymore."

"But, my dear, I need you to do this for me."

Catherine spun around. "For what? As your practical joke victim? No thank you."

"This is no joke, my dear. I know that I misled you with the portrait. At the time it didn't seem relevant for you to know that he was alive, but I truly do need you to show Lord Hildebrand around the city." Aunt Nellie's eyes turned pleading. "The poor man has special needs. You, with your love of London and training as a doctor, are perfectly suited to be his guide."

Catherine groaned and closed her eyes. She didn't know if she was more frustrated with him for being a male chauvinist or herself for having allowed herself to become so obsessed with his portrait. She'd even *dreamed* of him. With a sigh, she opened her eyes.

"What's wrong with him?" she asked.

"His Lordship has been dealing with some memory issues, mixing up things he studied as a youth but unable to recall more recent events."

"Has he had a brain injury?"

"He's seeking nontraditional care, and it's thought that this visit will help him." Aunt Nellie gave another pleading look at Catherine who thought she saw the flash of a twinkle. What did her hostess find humorous in this?

"Nontraditional? You mean like homeopathic?"

"My dear, he's very sensitive about it. You can imagine how a robust, virile man like him would feel devastated to have something like this happen. That's why I think it's best for you to be the one to take him around the city." Aunt Nellie let out a sad sigh.

"What's wrong with him?" Catherine whispered, feeling like she was in for a really bad holiday.

"I'm not at liberty to say. As I said, he's very sensitive about his condition." Aunt Nellie hurried on, "He's also lived quite a different life, and this is his first visit to London in many, many years. Please do this for me. I promise that if you will trust me and show the poor man some patience, you will come to understand. Just answer his questions . . . literally, as though it wasn't unusual that he doesn't know things."

Catherine heaved out a breath. She did feel bad for the man. Besides, how could she not enjoy taking someone around one of her favorite cities?

"I'll do it since I've already scheduled the time off."

"I do appreciate it, my dear. He needs to acclimatize and then I believe you two will get along famously." Aunt Nellie patted Catherine's arm comfortingly. "Now come back into the room so I may make formal introductions."

Aunt Nellie's fingers clasped Catherine's arm as though she might attempt to flee. When they entered the room, they found Gareth staring at the large portrait of the Americans. Something in his expression made Catherine think he recognized them. Interesting.

"My Lord," Aunt Nellie said, "I would like to introduce Dr. Catherine Ryan to you. Catherine, this is Lord Gareth Hildebrand—"

"Yes, I know that already." Catherine's irritation with him seemed out of proportion. It wasn't like she hadn't met lots of men like him, who thought all women should be there only to serve them.

Gareth turned a quizzical gaze at her. "You called me by my given name earlier. How do you know of me?"

"I answered before. Aunt Nellie told me about you." Catherine pointed to his painting.

The man glanced at Nellie, and she nodded.

"Now, my Lord," Aunt Nellie said, "I'm afraid I won't be able to take you around London during your stay. For the month, I'll be extremely busy with my house guests. They come here to participate in life as it was in the past. We call it a Regency Immersion Experience, and it's all the rage."

"Regency?" Gareth asked.

"You weren't just kidding, were you?" Catherine stared at her hostess for a second saying to him, "You do know your history, don't you? It's called the Regency era because it was the time period when George IV ruled as the Prince Regent. Where have you been all your life?"

"It's not necessary to be rude to the poor man." Aunt Nellie pinned Catherine with a disapproving scowl that made her face warm. "My guests wear clothing befitting the time. You, my Lord, should be able to mingle quite well, though I don't expect you to be spending much time here most days." Nellie shifted her gaze to Catherine. "Our good doctor has agreed to take time from her responsibilities to act as your guide during your stay."

He looked at Catherine warily, which made her feel even worse. He'd made one unfortunate comment to her, and now she was out to make him pay? She was better than that.

"As I'm sure you can tell," Aunt Nellie said, "Catherine speaks with an American accent. Her father was transferred to London when she was in her teens, and she has chosen to make this her home now. She's an A&E doctor."

"A&E?" he asked.

"It stands for 'accident and emergency,'" Aunt Nellie said, "and it's where people are treated who've been injured or are ill and cannot wait to be seen by their regular doctors."

"In the US we call it an ER. It stands for emergency room." Catherine felt a twinge of sympathy for the man. In many ways, he reminded her of a character in a Brendan Fraser movie about a man who'd been locked in a bomb shelter while the rest of the world had moved on without him. Catherine glanced at Aunt Nellie.

"My Lord," Nellie said, "the doctor knows that you're seeking help after your head injury, and that you suffer from some lapses in your memory."

Nellie gave him a meaningful glance, and he looked sincerely surprised. He gave a curt nod, his lips tight.

"My ball guests will just be going to dinner," Aunt Nellie said, indicating the door. "I believe your Lordship will feel better once you've had something to eat. Please escort the doctor since she is your dinner partner tonight. As for tomorrow morning, Catherine, I will have a car bring him to you at nine."

"What is this *car*?" he asked.

"A type of carriage," Aunt Nellie said simply and looked meaningfully at Catherine.

She nodded, accepting it to mean that was how Catherine should treat him.

Aunt Nellie then led the way from the room. The earl was silent and seemed fascinated by the electric lights. He stopped and reached up to touch one of the incandescent bulbs.

"Stop." Catherine grabbed his wrist. "You'll burn your fingers."

"Curious." He held his hand near it and nodded. "What is the fuel source?"

"Electricity."

"How does it work?"

"Sorry. I'm a doctor, not an electrical engineer. I'm just glad I can flip a switch and they work."

He gave a soft chuckle, and they continued to the dining room.

Gareth felt embarrassment to have fallen prey to the behavior Aunt Nellie had warned him about. The woman did see him as a country bumpkin, and he wished to change her opinion of him. He wasn't sure how to go about it in a place where female doctors were commonplace and lamps were powered by captured lightning. He'd attended Cambridge before his marriage but wouldn't have been considered an intellectual. He must keep quiet and learn more about this time.

Aunt Nellie signaled for him to join the line of guests slowly advancing toward the dining room.

"Great costume, man," a gentleman with an American accent said. "You must really get into this cosplay stuff. I admit I hadn't expected it to be this much fun when my wife first suggested we do this for our vacation this year." He turned away when the woman at his side spoke to him.

Cosplay? Reese had used unusual words or phrases. Like Gareth's sister, he'd assumed they were Americanisms. Once he'd understood she came from the future, he'd wondered if they referred to this time. Ellen had picked up a few of them and had begun her own cant at home. Rather than embarrass himself by showing his ignorance, he chose not to ask Catherine Ryan for clarification.

"Where did you receive your training to be a doctor?" he asked instead.

"Oxford."

"Did you?" Gareth forced his expression to remain neutral. "I attended Cambridge."

The doctor's expression turned dubious, but she said nothing. Was it that she didn't believe he'd attended there, or that it no longer existed? The idea that such an old and prestigious university might be gone gave him pause and made him question his desire to see so far into the future. It was unsettling in ways he hadn't anticipated when he'd petitioned Aunt Nellie for the boon.

For the first time, he also wondered what had motivated her to agree to it. She had been concerned enough that he might have a lapse of judgement to cast that *forgetful* magic on him. Why would she risk exposure? He wished he hadn't accepted her vague explanation about the magic telling her to send him.

And what of her warning that he must work *with* the magic? That implied that the magic would guide him while he was here. If so, how? And why? Her personification of the magic made him uneasy. He wished he had someone he could discuss this with, someone who could help him understand the implications. This future Nellie was similar yet different from the one in his time. He had no doubt she would be as evasive here, so he must find his answers elsewhere. But where?

He glanced at the doctor. She was an attractive woman. Like Reese, Catherine did not appear to be one to keep her opinions to herself, if their first meeting was any sign. Was it a trait of this age, this freedom of speaking one's thoughts? Did such license lead the ill-mannered to dictate behavior?

"You're very quiet, my Lord," the doctor finally said. "If it's because of something I've said, I need to apologize."

"I believe that's my responsibility," he said gravely. "I fear I set you against me when I discovered you were a physician. I truly do apologize for that. It may be common here but not so where I was raised. I should not have let my ignorance—"

"Be said out loud?" Catherine gave a soft chuckle, and it was a lovely sound. "Normally, I'm more diplomatic myself. I hope we can make a fresh start."

"I hope we may also."

She extended her hand. Did she mean for him to kiss it? Tentatively, he clasped it in his. Before he could pull it to his lips, she gave it a firm shake and took back her hand. Her cheeks flushed an attractive pink.

"I've been doing some research on excursions we can take," she said as they sat down to the meal. "After Aunt Nellie asked me to do it, I was able to mark off one extra day a week this month. I normally work three days. Do you have anywhere in mind that you'd like to visit while you're here?"

"I would enjoy a visit to the London Bridge. The ancient stonework is fascinating."

The doctor tilted her head, a crease between her brows, as though considering how to respond.

"That one was bought by an American and moved to Arizona," she finally said. "You can still see it, but you'll have to fly to the US."

Gareth's mouth went dry. Did anything he was familiar with remain? And what did she mean by flying? He was no bird.

"That's a beautiful dress," the man across from Catherine said.

At the appreciative way he looked at her, Gareth's hackles rose.

"It's not exactly era appropriate," the man said, apparently ignoring Gareth's glare.

"Since I'm not part of the immersion program, Aunt Nellie said it would be fine." Catherine turned to Gareth. "If you're into bridges, we have plenty of them. There's even a new London Bridge that opened in the seventies. If you like old bridges there's the Tower Bridge. It was built in the late 1800s, and I think it has a beautiful and distinctive design."

"I would enjoy seeing it."

"All right. When you were here before, did you see the Crown Jewels? I don't know when they opened them for public tours. They're pretty impressive. I'd hate to have to wear those crowns. It gives me a neck ache just to think about carrying all that weight on my head," Catherine said. "We could ride the London Eye, if you haven't gone on that before. It provides a nice view of the city if the weather's good. When you were here before, did you go on a cruise of the Thames?"

Gareth gave a noncommittal shrug. It would be a smelly proposition to sail that cesspool. Why would anyone choose to do that?

"Have *you* visited this London Eye?" he asked.

"Yes. If you're looking for an exciting ride, you'll be disappointed." She grinned, showing beautifully straight, white teeth. "When we first moved here, my father took the family on it. I thought it was going to be like riding a Ferris wheel back home."

He didn't know what a Ferris wheel was nor how to inquire about it. At his blank expression, a flash of sympathy crossed her face.

"Is it an entertaining attraction even if it is not exciting?" he finally asked.

"Like I said, it has a great view of the city."

With the weather being warmer there wouldn't be as much coal smoke. He realized then that the air didn't carry the smell of wood smoke from fireplaces.

"I would enjoy a view of the city," he said.

The meal was ending and guests were beginning to rise from the tables.

"I'm going to call it a night," Catherine said. "Be sure to wear comfortable shoes tomorrow. We can take the Tube, but we'll still be doing a lot of walking. Good night." She turned and left without a curtsy.

Gareth glanced around the room, wondering where Nellie planned to put him for the night.

"Are you ready to retire, my Lord?" a servant asked, appearing almost from nowhere. "Aunt Nellie has asked me to see to your needs. My name is Geoffrey."

"Are you to be my valet?"

"If that is what you require. Men today rarely need them." He indicated a door. "If you'll follow me, I'll take you to your chamber and introduce you to a wonderful modern convenience called the loo."

"Excellent." Gareth was interested in modern conveniences. He gave the room another glance. The entire assembly did have a more casual feel than those in his time. Tomorrow should be interesting.

5

THE VALET WOKE GARETH THE next morning at a country hour. Bleary from the late night and the after-effects of the time travel, he could remember only a scattering of things after dinner. He hoped the routine of being dressed, even by an unfamiliar valet, would relax him. He'd found the bed to be quite comfortable, and the soft sheets almost silk-like.

Several of the guests at the ball had held small objects in their hands and seemed to have been speaking into them. From their furtive glances, he supposed they must be modern items and not appropriate for the masquerade. Would they have been chastised had they been caught using them? He would have dearly loved to inquire about them but had chosen not to ask the doctor. She must believe him to be a candidate for Bedlam as it was.

"Before we get started, might I ask you a question?" Gareth asked of the valet.

"Of course, my Lord."

"I had intended to make this query of Aunt Nellie, but she seems to be avoiding me."

"She is quite busy this month, my Lord." The valet's tone had turned disapproving.

"Yes. But tell me about Reese and Mr. Taylor."

"They have wed, my Lord."

That had happened far faster than Gareth had expected. "Do you know if she is happy?"

"Aunt Nellie has shared Miss Clarisse's letters with the staff. She sounds very happy."

"Good. I truly am glad to hear it." And Gareth found he meant it.

"The first thing you must decide, my Lord," Geoffrey said, holding up two sets of smallclothes, "is if you prefer boxers or briefs." He then went into an explanation of the benefits of each. "If you find you don't like what you choose today, you may try another tomorrow."

Gareth would have preferred to wear what he knew. It must have shown in his expression.

"Aunt Nellie informed me that you are not an accidental traveler but that you chose this journey. Might I suggest that to fully appreciate the experience, you must immerse yourself in it as her guests do?"

Gareth nodded, accepting it as sound advice, though troubled that he hadn't reached that conclusion himself. He *had* been obsessed with seeing the future. He mustn't act like a debutante facing her first London Season.

"People today are much more casual in their clothing choices, frequently opting for comfort and ease of care," Geoffrey said.

"Yes, Aunt Nellie did mention that the pace of life is much faster than mine."

"Some might call it frenzied, my Lord, and I would agree. I will now introduce you to something called a zipper." The valet held up a pair of blue trousers with faded material.

"Has someone already worn these?" Gareth curled his lip in disgust.

"No, my Lord. It is considered fashionable to wear jeans—that is what these are called." He continued, "to wear jeans that have been *distressed*."

"So it's fashionable here to wear the castoff clothing of a common laborer?"

"Some of the most expensive styles have holes in them, by design, my Lord. As I said, comfort is frequently the key unless one is attending a special event and then all comfort is cast to the wind. These jeans—please remember to use the correct term—are of an expensive designer brand. 'Tis made of cotton, and you look like the locals."

Gareth peered more closely at the fabric, amazed at the perfectly straight stitches. He pinched the waist of the trousers between his fingers. The fabric was softer than he'd expected.

"Machines now make these, my Lord."

"Hence the consistency."

"Aye, my Lord." Geoffrey's voice pitched a little higher as his enthusiasm grew. "Now, let me show you how a zipper works. It has greatly increased the ease of dressing and has done away with much of the need for awkward buttons." He tugged on a tab, and the trousers opened. The valet pulled up on the tab, and the opening disappeared.

"Let me try that." Gareth took the garment and studied the teeth-like metal parts that held the two sections of the fabric together. "Clever."

"If you will now put them on, my Lord. You may find it easier if you sit." The valet indicated a chair. "They are close-fitting, so I would suggest you exercise caution the first time you close the zipper lest you pinch anything . . . tender."

Gareth chuckled at the man's delicacy. "If dressing is so much simpler now, why are there still valets?" he asked as he tried to slide one foot into the trousers.

"We are nearly obsolete, my Lord."

Gareth had to maneuver the fabric in order to get his foot

through the narrow leg opening. He pinched his lips. “How does this make it easier to dress?”

“One of the sacrifices made in the name of fashion, my Lord. Some ladies wear their jeans so tightly they give the appearance of having been painted on them.”

“*Ladies* wear these?” Gareth put his other foot into the jeans trousers.

“Aye, my Lord. I wanted to caution you before you left the house. You will see much today that will likely shock you. Skirts are worn above the knees, and some trousers are called ‘shorts’ because they also stop above the knees. Swimming attire covers little of the body. Some locations even sport nude beaches.”

While he considered the implications of this way of life, Gareth took his time sliding his foot the rest of the way through the leg. He thought back to the close-fitting outfit that Reese had worn to do her exercises. Was that a normal way people dressed now?

The casualness also made him wonder if there were even a distinction between the classes. Did his title exist in this time? It must, because the valet knew the proper way to address him.

“You should do the button first, my Lord,” the valet said when Gareth struggled to close the sections. “It will make drawing up the zipper easier.”

He did, and it slid easily into place. The jeans fit him snugly, and he looked to his man in query.

“They are tight now but will loosen with wear, my Lord.”

“When was this zipper tool invented?” Gareth asked.

“In the later 1800s. I remember it well,” Geoffrey said.

“How old *are* you?”

“Let us just say that I served as the valet for Master Jem, when Miss Clarisse visited Aunt Nellie’s for the first time.”

Gareth gaped and had to snap his mouth shut. His reasoning ability returned. If Aunt Nellie were still here, then of course her servants would be also.

Then the valet's remark sunk in. *When Miss Clarisse visited for the first time.* She must return to 1850. A thrill rushed through Gareth that he had to force down. He must focus on how happy such news would be to his sister. Ellen would be glad to see her friend again.

"This, my Lord, is called a polo shirt. It is patterned after an expensive designer label, but it is also comfortable and easy to put on. Remember that comfort is important to these people. Usually. They do insist upon extremes when dressing for parties or other special events, such as when the ladies wear outrageously high heels."

"I doubt I will attend any event requiring those," Gareth said, wondering what kind of shoes Catherine would wear. He would see her limbs if she wore her skirts above her knees.

"Breakfast will be brought to you, my Lord, as Aunt Nellie's guests dine in costume for their immersion experience. Have you decided if you wish to grow a beard during your stay, or if you would like to shave? Beards are all the rage at the moment."

"I would prefer to shave."

Geoffrey indicated the room with that clever "loo" device. "Then I believe you will enjoy another modern convenience, my Lord."

Catherine woke and had to think for a second what day of the week it was. She'd been having a lovely dream. It was a shame she couldn't recall what it had been about, just that she hadn't wanted it to stop. She rolled out of bed and was halfway to the shower before she remembered.

Gareth Hildebrand, the man she'd been thinking about for the past month, was *alive,* a real, breathing person and not a corpse rotting in his grave. A confusing, confused man she was going to spend the next few weeks with, taking him around to her favorite places in London.

As she showered, Catherine wished she understood her response to him. She was a logical woman. When she'd found herself curious about the man in the painting, sneaking to the fourth floor to study it, she'd put it off to being lonely. It'd been safe to fantasize about a man in a picture. Now she was faced with a living, breathing attractive man. A too-attractive man.

It'd been fun to play with fantasies of a guy from the past, with charming manners, someone who wasn't dangerous. In a lot of ways, he fit that image, but his memory challenges kept tripping her up. She hoped she wouldn't offend him when he surprised her with an odd comment. At the very least, it should be an interesting holiday break.

Catherine put a little too much thought into what she should wear. Part of her wanted to choose something pretty, which was ridiculous. She settled on simple jeans and a blouse. With her long hair pulled back in a ponytail and comfortable walking shoes, she was set to go.

She watched from her flat's window for the car to arrive. There was so much to see near where she lived that she didn't want to spend the day in traffic. He'd get to experience more while walking the city and riding the Tube. If he'd really not visited the city since his youth, she wondered how he'd gotten around. Did young earls take the Tube, or were they driven everywhere?

A car pulled up outside her building, and she recognized the driver as one of Nellie's servants. Catherine grabbed her purse and sunglasses before skipping down the stairs.

Gareth was just getting out of the car's rear door when she stepped outside.

"This is amazing," he said, pointing to the vehicle. "A horseless carriage. Did you know it has music?"

She couldn't help smiling. He reminded her of a child who'd just found out that Santa Claus was real. Gareth's enthusiasm was adorable, and she couldn't help being drawn to the man. She wished she could help him. For the first time since Aunt Nellie had asked Catherine to be his tour guide, she was looking forward to it. His enthusiasm would make it a delight to take him around the city.

She realized he was gawking at her now. He coughed and dropped his gaze.

"My apologies. I didn't mean to stare," Gareth said. "You wear those quite well."

A flush went through her, and tried not to think about it. So what if he found her attractive.

"I don't think I've met you before," she said, extending her hand to the driver, who stood by the car. "I'm Catherine Ryan."

"Dr. Ryan. My name is Walter." He shook her hand.

"I've emailed Aunt Nellie our itinerary. Today, the earl and I will be doing a lot of walking," Catherine told the driver, who stood by the car. She said to Gareth, "Do you walk much where you're from?"

"A fair amount, though I ride more."

Did he mean riding a motorcycle? Catherine couldn't imagine him on a scooter and definitely not a moped. Did he mean a *horse*?

"It's not a problem. If you're not on your feet a lot like I am, you could end up with blisters and sore muscles. That's why I'm alternating between walking days and bus excursions." She turned back to the driver. "We'll walk this morning, but I'd like you to pick us up after lunch please. Could you give me your number in case we need you to get us sooner?"

"Of course." The man held out his mobile, and she typed her number into it.

"Ring me so I have your number." When Walter did, she said, "Perfect. I'll let you know if we need you sooner."

"As you say." The man bowed to the earl. "My Lord."

Gareth gave a nod of acknowledgment and came to stand beside her.

"What was that you just did?" he asked when the car had pulled away.

"We exchanged mobile numbers."

Gareth stilled in a way that was already becoming familiar. He hadn't understood the reference.

"It's so I can contact Walter from wherever we're at."

"May I?" Gareth pointed to her mobile, so she handed it to him. He turned it over like he'd never seen one before and asked, "What is it?"

"It's a device that reproduces sounds at a distance and is a way to communicate," she said kindly. "When they were first invented, they were connected with wires. Now they use cellular towers to transmit the sound waves. That's why, in America, we call them cell phones. Here, we call them mobile phones because they let us talk to people while we're on the move."

"Mobile phone." Gareth nodded and mouthed the words again. It reminded her of someone who was trying to learn another language. Maybe that's exactly what it was like for him.

"Didn't you ever string cans together to talk to your friends when you were a kid? My mother did."

He shook his head, a crease appearing between his brows.

"It's not a problem. I didn't either." Catherine guessed he wouldn't know what a telly was either. How interesting that he was able to remember the meaning of some words but not others. She'd love to talk with whoever was treating him. "We use telecommunications to share information. There are towers all over the city to relay the signals. When we take a river cruise on the Thames, I'll point out the BT Tower that was built in the sixties and is still used today."

Gareth only nodded, once again reminding her of people who didn't speak the language and nodded as a defensive mechanism to hide their embarrassment. She'd never considered before how much technical jargon was mingled in the English language. She thought that if her great grandmother were still alive, she'd have as much trouble understanding Catherine as this poor man did.

A random thought made her blink, and she narrowed her eyes, studying him. He really was like a blast from the past.

"Doctor, is something amiss?" he asked.

"No, but that reminds me." She took his arm and pulled him closer to her apartment building to let a woman pushing a pram pass by. "I would prefer you not refer to me by my title. Call me Catherine."

"That is not appropriate." Gareth's tone had turned disapproving, but he frowned and added, "Where I live."

"Well, you'll stand out if you don't, so please call me Catherine, and I'll call you Gareth." When he looked about to argue, she added, "I know this city. That's why Aunt Nellie's asked me to show you around. You have to believe that I also know of potential dangers that you don't, including people who might think it's funny to jump a member of the peerage. If I were to visit your home, I would have to trust you to keep me safe."

He held her gaze for a second and then gave a single nod. "I give you my trust."

The simplicity of those words struck Catherine. She recognized that, in speaking them, this eighth earl of Kellworth had conceded something to her that was very important to him. Giving in on this was no small thing. The thought made her eyes sting. She blinked, embarrassed at the sudden emotion. How ridiculous.

"Thank you, Gareth," she said.

"It is my pleasure," he replied, his eyes now taking on a twinkle, "Catherine."

"Have you eaten breakfast?"

"Yes."

"Well, I haven't," she said. "There's a pastry shop up the street, so I'd like to stop there first."

Gareth held out his arm, so she took it and had to push down a fluttery feeling like she'd had when she'd woken up that morning. Catherine wondered if she'd been dreaming about *him*.

"I'm used to carrying a cane, when I walk about town," Gareth said, "but I failed to bring mine with me. By chance will it be possible to find one?"

"Sure." His statement, while unexpected, also didn't surprise her. The image of him walking along the London streets with a cane, like a well-bred man of the past, seemed to fit him. It might make him stand out but not scream that he was a member of the peerage. She said, "I know of a little shop on the way to the bakery that might have just what you're looking for."

When they reached it, Gareth strode straight in and went to the wall where a number of canes were displayed. From the prices on some of them, Catherine guessed they must be antiques.

"I have realized what's been missing from the men on the streets," Gareth said, glancing over his shoulder. "No one carries canes or swords. Or wears hats."

"That's because if they carried swords they'd probably be arrested. It's against the law," she said, bemused. "The police usually only carry batons and not guns like in America."

"Hmm. This one looks promising." Gareth tilted a simple but elegant cane and then twisted it around like he might have a sword, wearing a slight frown. "That is strange."

"What is it?" Catherine stepped beside him, curious.

"It's heavier than it should be on this end." He handed it to her. It was a *lot* heavier on the thick end. She gave it back to him, and he examined the metal tip. "Usually, these are brass or silver, but this appears to be steel."

"Is that significant?" Catherine leaned closer. He smelled yummy. *Stop that.*

"I believe it's not only the tip that is steel but a rod in the middle." Gareth shifted his grip on the cane several times, finally settling with his hand about a foot from the base. He stepped away from her and made some graceful defensive-like moves. "Yes, though it doesn't appear to run the full length of the shaft. It will make a much sturdier cane and could provide a defensive weapon should that be needed. This will do." He looked at her and grinned.

He was *so* cute.

"Nice moves, but do you expect to *need* a defensive weapon?" she asked a little weakly. What was he going to come up with next?

"One never knows and should be prepared for anything." Gareth signaled the clerk who was watching them a little warily. "I will take this. You may put it on the tab of—"

"I've got it." Catherine rushed forward before he could announce his title to the world.

Gareth watched with interest as she pulled out her debit card and paid for the cane.

"I will settle my accounts before I return home," he said.

"That's something you can talk to Aunt Nellie about." Catherine put the receipt in her purse.

"I will."

"You looked like you know what you're doing with that thing," she said once they were back on the street. "Do you fence?"

"Of course." He held out his arm to her again, and she took it. "Most gentlemen study it in school. I'm quite good at it, if I say so myself."

"Have you boxed?" At his blank expression, she reached for the old-fashioned word. "Fisticuffs?"

"Pugilism? No. That's no longer considered appropriate for gentlemen."

"I'm surprised you'd say that," Catherine said. "I read recently that boxing in England is coming into another golden age. I'm not a fan myself, but it's less brutal than cage fighting."

His expression had gone blank. Something else he didn't remember. She decided trying to explain the violent mixed martial art would lead to more questions that she'd rather not go into.

As they made their way to the pastry shop, most of the stores caught Gareth's interest. She didn't try to walk fast, even though her stomach was growling, because he seemed fascinated by each business and had to stop to look at everything.

She smiled at him indulgently. At this rate, they'd be lucky to get to Big Ben by lunchtime.

Gareth forced himself not to limp as he continued walking at Catherine's pace. He would not allow her to outdo him though his calves ached fiercely. His head was still reeling from everything that he'd seen. Everyone seemed to be in a hurry, rushing hither and thither.

"Let's stop here." She gestured to a bench. "I think you need a break."

"Only if you do." It took all his control not to groan as he sat beside her.

"I'm sorry. You should have said something sooner." She took a bottle from her bag and handed it to him.

"What's this?"

"Open it for me." She reached over and lifted his leg to her lap.

"What are you doing?" he gasped, struggling as she forced up the leg of his jeans.

"I'm going to work out the knots in your leg. Now stop it." She pinned him with a stern look, worthy of anything Nurse had given him as a boy.

Catherine held out her hand for the bottle and he set it in her palm. She shot him a flat look.

"What?"

"Pour a little in my hand."

Gareth retrieved the small bottle and poured some of the liquid into her palm. A pleasant minty fragrance drifted up. As she spread it over his shin and calf, his entire body flushed, only part of it from embarrassment. Never before had a woman touched him in such a familiar manner that had not also involved intimacy and certainly not in public. He ducked his head and glanced from the corner of his eye to see if people were watching them. No one paid them any heed.

Catherine's fingers started kneading the muscles. He groaned, first with pain and then with pleasure. She glanced up at him, her hands still working, and grinned.

"One of my college roommates was attending massage therapy school and used to practice on us. It's something that comes in handy, so I had her teach me some simple techniques. Believe me, I've spent some very long days on my feet and have had to use this on myself. That's why I carry that bottle around with me."

"What is massage therapy?" Gareth closed his eyes when she hit a tender knot in his shin and grimaced as she worked it out.

"It's manipulation of the soft tissues and muscles. It helps with circulation too. I had an elderly neighbor who had such bad blood flow in her legs that the skin was turning black. She couldn't afford to pay for regular massages so I gave them to her a couple of times a week. I had the skin on her legs looking pink and healthy again in a few months." Catherine slid his leg off her lap. "Arch your foot."

Gareth did. While it was still sore, he could move it again. "This is beyond anything I've experienced."

"I agree. Now let's do your other leg."

"Is the old woman no longer your neighbor?" he asked, lifting it to her lap.

"She got too old to live on her own, and her kids put her in a home."

"You don't approve?"

"Well, my parents taught me a different way. We moved to England so my father could care for his mother."

Gareth approved. Family took care of its own. That was why Grandmama was moving from Bath to the dower house, so they could better see to her needs. He watched Catherine work, wondering what had made her wish to study medicine.

"Was your father also a doctor?" he asked.

"Oh, no. He fainted at the sight of blood." She gave a soft chuckle but there was a hint of sadness with it.

"Tell me what is involved to become a doctor."

Gareth listened as she spoke of her years of study and training. He doubted he would be able to think of doctoring the same way again. There was certainly more involved than giving out powders and bloodletting.

"That should do it," she said, resting her hands on his leg.

He arched the foot and smiled. "You, dear doctor, are a miracle worker."

"Ah. Get on with you." Catherine took back her bottle and returned the cap. "I don't know about you, but I'm starved. There's a nice restaurant not far from here. Have you had enough of me? You can have Walter take you back to Twickenham or get a bite to eat with me."

"I would much prefer to share a meal with you."

She shot him a quick glance but seemed pleased and stood, slinging her backpack over one shoulder.

Gareth rose and alternately arched his feet. "Truly. You are a miracle worker."

Catherine waggled her fingers. "Magic hands." She nodded across the park.

Gareth recognized the shop where he'd purchased his cane that morning. Perhaps he would eventually be able to find his way around the city on his own. Not that he wished to. He was finding that he enjoyed Catherine's company. Very much. He offered her his arm, and she wrapped her fingers around it.

"What was your childhood like?" she asked as they headed out of the park.

Gareth decided to tell her about the formidable woman he'd called Nurse.

6

GARETH PRESENTED HIMSELF AT THE car early, quite pleased for having dressed and shaved himself. The modern clothing styles did lend themselves to it. While he still preferred his buckskin breaches, the jeans trousers had become more comfortable the longer he'd worn them. He had definitely enjoyed the way Catherine's had fit her curvy form. The manner of dress among masses, clad so skimpily, had shocked him at first. Compared to some, her tight trousers had been conservative.

"You're here early this morning, my Lord," Walter said, approaching the Twickenham car. "I hope I haven't kept you waiting." He pressed the key device and opened the back door for Gareth.

"Not at all. I merely find this time enthralling and am anxious to begin my day." He slid into the back seat.

"Well, my Lord, you seem to be more comfortable." Walter brought the carriage to life.

"Indeed." Gareth chuckled softly. "I confess that yesterday was a bit overwhelming. I spent most of the night sorting it all in my mind."

"What have you found the most interesting, my Lord?" The driver looked back through the odd mirror.

"There is so much. I confess that at first I gawked too much. Nellie had cautioned me not to behave that way, so I did overcome it rather quickly, I believe. Though perhaps Catherine can speak to that more honestly than I." Gareth glanced out the window, studying the other cars on the street as they sped along. "The changes have left me thinking a great deal."

"How so, my Lord?"

"You are a man who has lived in my time. Once, catching a glimpse of a woman's ankle was considered tantalizing."

Walter chuckled and nodded his head.

"While we strolled this part of the city yesterday, I often had to avert my gaze. *Me.* As though I were visiting a low-end London neighborhood where brothels abounded."

"Are you a frequent visitor to those parts of town in your day, my Lord?" Walter asked, his tone teasing.

Gareth straightened in his seat, ready to chastise the driver. Then the cheeky man had the nerve to wink at him.

"It's a different time, my Lord, but I do apologize if I have offended you."

"Take care, Walter. I'm still a peer."

"True enough, my Lord. But as you were saying?"

"Merely that the people of this time wear their 'short' clothing so casually, even naturally, that after viewing so many exposed limbs and the occasional bared stomach I found my sensitivity to it dulled. By the time I returned to Twickenham Manor, I'd seen so many women's bare ankles that I no longer paid heed to them. I find it curious that covering a part of the body has the power to add to its allure."

"It is an odd part of human nature. Tell people they can't have something, and they immediately want it."

Gareth thought back to the "exercise" clothing he'd seen Reese wear one time. His sister had lately insisted upon having a costume made for herself to wear, so she could continue the strengthening movements she'd been taught during Reese's stay. When he'd tried to argue with her that a woman had no need to be strong, Ellen had reminded him of the time when Reese had needed her strength to protect herself from guests at Kellworth.

His sister had insisted that she would also be strong. Gareth had never seen Ellen so forceful. When he'd understood how much she'd set her heart on the garment, he'd given in to her demands. He was simply grateful that the exercise clothing she now wore covered her person. His only demand, and what he'd refused to back down on, was that she had to agree to only wear them inside the house when there were no guests who might see her.

"Do all women of this time wear special exercise clothing?" he asked.

"Many do because the exercise fabrics have more stretch to them, so they're more comfortable."

Gareth wondered if Catherine took exercise. Did she, like many people, run down the streets with strange wires coming from her ears? She'd called them *joggers* and said they were probably listening to music.

"You should try it sometime, my Lord."

"Try what?"

"Exercising. You might ask the good doctor about it."

"Perhaps I will."

"Has anything impressed you about this city now as opposed to what it was like in your time?"

"I think perhaps the most striking thing for me has been the improvement to the Thames."

"Aye, my Lord," Walter said. "It's something that was changed only in the last sixty years or so. Back then, the Natural History Museum declared it to be biologically dead."

"Biologically dead?"

"It means there wasn't enough oxygen—" The driver

frowned. "There wasn't enough of what fish need to live there, my Lord. The German bombing during World War II damaged many of the Victorian sewers. All that waste ended up in the river. Post-war England didn't have the wherewithal to fix it right away."

"World War *II*? What does that mean?" Gareth's stomach knotted at the implication.

"I'm sad to say a great number of terrible things have befallen the world since your time, my Lord. If you're interested in learning more, I would suggest you ask Catherine to take you to one of the many museums in the city." Walter glanced at him through the mirror again. "Sadly, the terrible things that still happen are nothing new. As you well know, the gruesome tortures mankind has committed go back for centuries, as can be seen in the dungeons of many English castles."

Gareth sat quietly for the rest of the trip to Catherine's lodging, lost in his thoughts. He'd observed enough of this time to know it was no utopia, but *world wars*? Was this what his descendants had to look forward to?

"My apologies, my Lord, if I have put you out of sorts," Walter said as he opened Gareth's door.

"You have merely given me much to think upon." Remembering how he'd said those same words to Reese made him give a dark chuckle. Now that he'd seen a glimmer of the world she lived in, he finally understood her passion to make it a better place. His pride increased at his sister's desire to do the same.

Catherine waited on her doorstep, watching him, her brows knit.

"Is something wrong?" she asked.

"No, my dear. I'm merely still considering what I've learned." He bowed. "I didn't break my fast before leaving today and look forward to visiting your pastry shop today to sample their wares."

"Good plan."

"I will await your ring," Walter said, opening his door.

"I hadn't thought before how that might disrupt your schedule," Catherine said to the driver. "I'm sorry."

"Have no concern. Aunt Nellie has asked me to stay nearby in case you have need of me quickly. That's why she wanted a copy of your itinerary." He returned to the car.

Catherine turned to Gareth, and he extended his arm to her. This time, when she wrapped her fingers around his arm, he covered her hand with his. She twitched a little under his touch but didn't withdraw. That lifted his spirits immensely, and he had to bite back a smile. The more time he spent with this woman, the more fascinating she became.

"I hope your feet got a good rest last night. What have you enjoyed the most so far?" she asked as they merged with the busy foot traffic.

"I thoroughly enjoyed seeing Big Ben and the Palace of Westminster." Gareth couldn't help smiling. In his time, construction had begun to rebuild the burned palace at Westminster. It amused him that he had seen the now-aged but completed clock tower and home of Parliament.

"What are you grinning about?" Catherine asked.

Gareth experienced a powerful desire to tell her the truth. The words were on the tip of his tongue when he recalled the price he would pay if he spoke them.

"What pastries would you recommend that I consider?" he asked instead, pointing to the shop's window a few paces ahead.

She shot him a flat look at his change in topic, but he said nothing. He dared not risk losing his new purpose in life, and that came from his memories of Reese.

They chose their pastries and stepped out of the shop. Never in his time would the Quality have strolled while eating. One simply didn't do that on the street. However, he had seen many people eat "on the run" as Catherine had called it, so apparently it wasn't uncommon now.

"You're thinking again," she said, tearing off the corner of her fruit pasty. "Why won't you tell me?"

"I have certain restrictions about what I may disclose. It's obvious to you that I am different."

"Yes, you're probably the most unusual man I've ever met."

Her words should have troubled him. At home, one must fit into the accepted mode, and he was a man very much a part of his class, a member of the Ton who was invited to the best parties. Being unusual would not have been accepted in his time. That was what had appealed to him about Reese, her uniqueness compared to his female acquaintances. Catherine had the same feistiness.

"Is that good?" he asked.

"Maybe." She gave him one of her considering glances. "You sometimes play the male chauvinist, but you're also willing to consider a different way of thinking. I like that."

"I'm not familiar with that expression, male chauvinist."

Catherine pinched her brows. "It's a man who thinks women are inferior."

"You believe I think you inferior?"

"If not, why would you be surprised that I'm a doctor?"

"My response was one of surprise and not of disbelief that a female *could* be a doctor," Gareth lied, sensing that he must take care with his answer. "Where I live there simply are none, so it has never occurred to me that any would wish to be."

Something flashed across her expression, but Catherine said no more about it, pointing instead to a building they'd passed the day before. Did his odd comments cause her to hold herself back and not share more about herself with him?

"We'll be taking the Tube today."

Gareth let out a breath. "Again, I must demonstrate my ignorance by asking what this Tube is."

The corner of her eye twitched, as it had taken to doing when he should know something but didn't. Truly, what had Aunt Nellie been thinking to assign him someone from this time to be his guide? Walter, for example, could have easily shown the sights. His schedule was already tied to Gareth's. Though he had to admit that he enjoyed Catherine's company.

He did, however, sometimes wonder if his hostess might have created a situation where he couldn't help but betray himself as a traveler of time. Did she hope to claim he'd breached his agreement with her?

"The Tube is the underground railway system," Catherine said.

"Ah, I *do* know of that. I visited with other members of the House of Lords—" he broke off before he could say that he'd visited the Wapping Station, when it had first opened. "So you call it the Tube."

"Yes," she said. "You've seen how busy the streets are. Imagine if eight million people tried to get around on those alone. When we moved here from America, it's the thing that impressed me the most. It's so easy to get around the city."

"Such a far-reaching view." Many of Gareth's London servants didn't live in his house there but went to their own homes at night, especially the ones with families. He hadn't considered how difficult that might be for them.

"One of the first things we have to do is get your Oyster card."

Not wanting to set that twitch going again, he said nothing as Catherine went to a machine and used a rectangular card, as she had done yesterday. She quickly pressed her fingers against words on the panel.

"This way." She handed him a blue and white card made of a curious material with the word Oyster on it. "I got you one with fifty pounds on it. If you have any money left over on the card, you can give it to Nellie for someone else to use since she paid for it."

Gareth's step faltered. She'd paid *fifty pounds* for him? He must speak to Aunt Nellie about it. Glancing around, he realized Catherine had moved far ahead. He had to make haste before he lost sight of her in the crowd. What if someone accosted her?

When she used the Oyster card at a barrier, the bar blocking forward movement shifted, allowing her to pass through. It closed before he could do the same.

"Put your card here." When he did, the bar moved, and Catherine added, "We'll do this again at our destination, and the charge will be deducted from the card. Brilliant, right?"

"As you say." Gareth glanced back at the barrier.

"This way." Catherine took his hand.

Bemused, he curled his fingers around hers and allowed her to lead him through a labyrinth of stairs and corridors full of people. Finally, they stepped into what was essentially a tube-shaped room, and he understood the name.

The close proximity of so many people put him on edge that unsavory characters might be lurking among them, and he pulled her nearer to him. It was then that he noticed her breathing had become somewhat irregular.

"Are you well?" he asked, concerned.

"I'll be fine." She let out a breath. "Good plan to stay close so we're not separated. We're going to the Waterloo Station. It's only a few minutes to the Eye and the dock."

"What are we doing at—" Gareth broke off as a train pulled up. The doors opened, apparently without human assistance, and people poured out. As soon as they were clear, the crowd in the station pressed forward to enter it. He stared, slack-jawed.

Catherine pulled him into the train.

"The doors close quickly," she said, clasping a metal pole with her free hand.

Gareth frowned at a young man who continued to sit nearby, giving no indication that he meant to rise and give his seat to a lady.

"How dare you sit while a lady stands," Gareth said in his sternest voice.

"I'm fine." Catherine's cheeks had flushed, and she waved at the youth to stay seated. She lifted on her tiptoes and whispered in Gareth's ear, "Men don't often give up their seats for women anymore. Equal rights and all that. Don't worry about it."

"Equal rights?" he repeated, aware of her closeness, her flowery fragrance filling his senses.

Catherine gave him one of her considering looks but only said, "Women wanted the law to recognize that they were full citizens, just like men, and the freedom to make decisions for themselves."

"Freedom," he said, his words soft.

Gareth hadn't thought of his sister's position in those terms. It'd been his responsibility to watch over her for nearly a decade. He would never have forced her to marry someone she didn't want to, but he couldn't say their father wouldn't have pressured her into accepting what he considered an advantageous offer.

He'd been raised to believe that women were weaker and men needed to protect and care for them. Gareth thought back to the day before. Had he seen signs of the kind of solicitous care he would expect in his time? Yes, he thought so. It *was* there in some people, though subtler, such as a couple walking up the busy street. The man had moved his female companion to the inside of the walkway so he stood between her and the traffic. Just as any gentleman should.

"This is our stop." Catherine took his arm this time, apparently unaware of the ideas she'd stirred in him.

Gareth was quite pleased that he didn't need help using the Oyster card as they exited the station. Only then did he remember that he had a question.

"What powers the trains?" he asked.

"Electricity."

There was that electricity again. What an amazingly versatile thing. He wondered what was involved with capturing and harnessing it for use.

"This way to our first stop." Catherine nodded to a sign that said *London Eye*.

7

THEY'D TIMED IT PERFECTLY TO queue up for the ride. Catherine wondered what she could have said that had turned Gareth so thoughtful. He seemed really preoccupied this morning, and she hoped she hadn't done anything to offend him. She found she enjoyed his quirky sense of humor, and she missed his odd questions.

Since he didn't seem to want to talk, Catherine chatted with an American family while they waited in line. Finally, it was their turn to enter a capsule. She grinned when they began to slowly rise.

As always, the view fascinated her, and she stepped to the glass. Catherine would never forget the first time she'd seen the city from there. She hoped Gareth was enjoying it.

Glancing back, she was surprised to find him standing rigidly in the center, one white-knuckled hand clutching his cane. She understood then.

"I'm so sorry, Gareth." Catherine went to him and slid her hand into his, surprised at how cold it was. She asked, softly, "Are you afraid of heights?"

"I had not thought so." He gave her a tight smile, the muscles of his jaw twitching, the pulse quick in his neck. The poor man looked like he was determined not to show cowardice. How stupid of her not to have considered this.

She let go of his hand and slid her arms around his waist. He didn't hesitate to pull her against him in a tight embrace that was almost uncomfortable. His heart was beating so fast, she wondered what his blood pressure was. She needed to see if she could calm him down.

"It's such a beautiful day," Catherine said in an attempt to distract him, her cheek against his shoulder as they faced the view. It was going to be a very long thirty minutes. "Did I ever tell you how I fell in love with this city as soon as I stepped off the plane? In America, we think things are old after two or three hundred years. London's about two *thousand* years old.

"Have you been to Southwark Cathedral? It's not far from the new London Bridge. The Cathedral was constructed in the fifteenth century, and it's still an active parish. I mean, Christopher Columbus didn't even get to America until the end of the fifteenth century. It took my breath away the first time I saw it and realized I was walking in the same place that Chaucer and Shakespeare had stood."

As Catherine continued to ramble on about her first experiences with the city, Gareth's grip on her eased a little, and his breathing relaxed. The sound of his heartbeat against her ear softened as it slowed.

Almost of their own accord, her hands ran up his back, feeling the strong muscles. She inhaled deeply, enjoying his masculine scent, the feel of his arms about her. A powerful attraction washed through her, and she glanced up to find him watching her. His gaze was intense, his eyes dilated with desire, and his heart had started racing again. When he looked at her mouth, she thought he might kiss her.

That was wrong. She dropped her hands and stepped back, her whole body hot. Catherine had only known him for a couple of days and shouldn't be encouraging something like that anyway. She wasn't ready to get involved again, and he was leaving in a month.

"Thank you," he said, his voice soft. "I've never been so far off the ground, so my response to the height was unexpected."

"My pleasure." Catherine's cheeks flamed, and he chuckled, seemingly unconcerned with their too-intimate moment. Did that mean he did that kind of thing a lot? Was he a player? She hated the thought and searched for something to change the subject. "We should take a selfie."

"A what?" he asked.

"I can take your picture," one of the Americans offered.

"Thank you. Do it with Westminster behind us, please." Catherine handed over her mobile and signaled Gareth to turn. She took up position beside him and whispered, "Smile and look at the mobile."

"One. Two. Three," the American said. "And again. Here. Check to make sure they're not blurry."

Catherine took the mobile and brought up the picture. Beside her, Gareth gasped.

"Should I take another?" the American woman asked.

"No, they turned out great. Thank you." Catherine waited until the woman had returned to her group before asking Gareth, "What's wrong?"

"May I look at that again?" Gareth indicated her phone. She found the photo and handed the mobile to him. "This is . . . incredible. How is this possible?"

At her expression, he flushed.

"You look very beautiful," he said, and it was her turn to color.

The capsule came to a stop then, for which Catherine was grateful, and the people started moving toward the exit. Gareth held out his arm to her, and she hesitated. Not wanting to make their earlier moment a big deal, she slipped her mobile into her purse and wrapped her fingers around his bicep.

She seemed to be more aware now of how strong he was, and she had to force back the memory of holding him. Oh dear, she was in trouble. He covered her hand with his, and she winced. She liked it too much, liked *him*.

That's what came of obsessing over his portrait for a month and then meeting him in person. Catherine had set herself up for this response. It wasn't real.

They were quiet as they made their way to the dock. After the height experience, she was second guessing the speedboat tour.

"Where are we off to now?" he asked.

"Well, I have tickets for a boat ride, but it depends," she said. "How are you feeling?"

"Now that we're on the ground again, I've never felt better."

She didn't think she imagined his hand tightening over hers a little, as though he were telling her that *she* was making him feel that way. What a flirt.

"Behave, Gareth," Catherine muttered, and he chuckled. Definitely a tease. Maybe he deserved the ride on a speedboat. She pointed to the river. "It's right over there."

As they strolled toward the dock, she said, "I wanted to remind you that I have to work for three days, so you'll be on your own."

"So Aunt Nellie has informed me." He didn't look very happy. "Will I see you in the evenings?"

"I work long days, and I'm tired when I get home. I gave her a list of some places you might like to visit. Didn't she show it to you?"

"Yes. She informed me that Walter would be available to drive me."

"But?"

"I will wait until you are able to show me. She said there is something called the internet that I can read. It is similar to the newspaper." Gareth sounded pleased with himself for knowing that.

"Just don't trust everything you read there. Here we are."

He was quiet as she signed them in and they walked up the long pier. When she gave him a life vest, he asked, "What is this for?"

"It's a flotation device in case the boat sinks." When he frowned, she had to bite back a smile. "It's just a precaution. Don't worry. I ride these at least once a year, and there's never been a problem."

Gareth needed a little help getting the belt to clip, and then played with it a few times, clasping and unclasping it, like he'd never seen a plastic buckle before. Sometimes he was like a little kid.

"Leave it," Catherine finally said, covering his hand with hers. He gave her a cheeky grin, and she wondered if he'd done it on purpose so she'd touch him. *"Gareth,"* she growled.

"This way," one of the staff members said.

They boarded the craft, and Catherine went for the second seat from the front. She wanted to make sure they had something to hang on to.

"Have you been boating on the Thames before?" she asked.

A disgusted look crossed his face, and he shook his head.

"Then you're in for a real treat." She gave him a sly grin, and he narrowed his eyes, wary. She said, "Just wait."

In spite of Walter's earlier description of the Thames, Gareth was impressed by how greatly it had been improved. He would have cringed at the thought of taking a boat into the river's water in his day. The revolting image made him shudder a little.

Disconcertingly, it also made him recall that repulsive sewer that had once run between the homes of one of his tenant villages. Before Reese had stepped in to change things.

"The last time I visited London," he said, "such a thing would not have been considered."

Spending so much time in Catherine's company had driven home to him how important it was to be as honest as he could, otherwise he was sure to be caught in the lie. As he became better acquainted with her, he found he liked her quite a bit, the spark of attraction tantalizing. He had to remind himself that he could flirt with her, but she was not a woman to be trifled with.

"I hope this ride isn't a mistake," Catherine muttered and then said more loudly, "I love to do this. It's one of my favorite things. Someday I'd like to go on a cruise."

"And what is that?" He knew as soon as he spoke the word that it was something that a man in this time would have known.

"Either an ocean cruise or one of the river cruises. One part of my mother's family comes from Germany, and I think it'd be fun to check out some of the cities along the Rhine."

"I do not wish to show my ignorance, but I still do not understand," Gareth said after a pause. Since he had begun this, he might as well finish it.

"What don't you understand?" she asked.

"What is a cruise?"

The question set off Catherine's twitch, but it passed quickly. If he had not become so familiar with her lovely face, he doubted he would have noticed it.

She impressed him with how discrete she had learned to be at times like this. Her look was not devoid of surprise but rather showed a diplomatic finesse now. He could not imagine anyone in his day taking his questions so well. Catherine's expression lacked the irritation that he had often seen on Reese's face.

With that observation, he accepted that she would have struggled to fit into his social set, might have even been a detriment to the work he hoped to do. He valued how her crusader determination had wakened him to what he could accomplish, but she would not have made a good partner in the subtler world of politics.

Catherine gave a soft cough, pulling him from his ruminations.

"A cruise," she said, "is essentially a floating resort in the form of a ship. People take holidays on them because it's actually an economical way to visit fun places."

A ship resort. Gareth nodded thoughtfully, frowning as he tried to imagine holding the kinds of social functions he was required to attend during the London Season while on a floating resort.

"You mentioned taking an *ocean* cruise."

Catherine gave a soft chuckle. "I'm guessing you've never been on one."

The people of this time must spend holidays on a ship for pleasure. Incomprehensible.

"No, indeed not," he said. "Ocean voyages are a means for traveling to distant locations, such as America. It's a lengthy and, from what I understand, uncomfortable method of transportation."

"If it's only for getting from point A to point B," Catherine said, "it'd be better to go by plane."

He stilled but kept his expression neutral. She'd used that word before, but he had no idea what it was. A flash of humor crossed her face that made him think she understood.

"What?" he asked.

"I get it." Catherine put her hand over his for a second, and the warmth spread up his arm. "I remember what it was like to be new to a place where people use words that sound like they ought to be familiar but obviously have a different connotation." She pulled back her hand, and her voice turned wistful. "If you ever have the opportunity to take a luxury cruise, do it. I think you'd enjoy it. Someday, I'll get to."

Gareth wished he had the power to make her wish happen. He thought he would enjoy going on a grand adventure at sea with her as a companion.

"Since you don't cruise," she said, "what *do* you like to do?"

"I enjoy many activities. I have not considered it of late."

"Why not?"

"I had sufficient responsibilities in both the winter and the summer to occupy most of my time. I have a younger sister who is in my care."

"Oh, do you?" Catherine shifted and gazed upon him with interest. "What's her name? How old is she? What's she like?"

"Her name is Ellen, and she will come of age in a few months. I've had the responsibility of her since our father died of the cancer when she was eleven."

"I'm sorry you two lost your parents." Catherine's expression turned sympathetic, but it had also darkened with something else.

"I surmise that you have also lost your parents." Gareth covered her hand this time, and she gave a faint smile.

"Yes. And so much more. Is your sister like you?"

"Oh, no. She is a much better person than I." Unlike Gareth, his sister had been the first to embrace Reese and her desires to do good. He'd had to be shamed into it.

Catherine shot him a curious look, but their guide, who had stopped his presentation to answer some questions, started in again, and they gave their attention to him. Gareth should not have found it surprising that the two of them, separated by decades, gender, and culture, shared something that had touched them so deeply.

"I enjoy riding and most outdoor activities I suppose." Gareth gave a little shrug. "I have recently discovered that I find pleasure in seeking ways to assist people to make their lives better." He thought whimsically of Reese's influence in that, but he then saw Catherine watching him. He asked, "And you?"

"I like to read."

"Do you stay abreast with local politics?"

"Well, I watch the news, if that's what you mean."

"Ah, yes, those people who talk to you from that box. I believe my valet called it a telly."

Gareth scanned the buildings, shaking his head, unable to think of an adequate way to describe the assortment of oddly-shaped structures. Even in his fanciful youth when he'd enjoyed reading the works of Hans Christian Andersen or Washington Irving, Gareth doubted he would have ever imagined anything like this.

"I must say, the architecture is . . ." His words trailed off.

"An eclectic blend of styles?" she asked.

"Well said. Yes, that is it exactly."

He met her gaze, struck that she had chosen the words he would have used to describe them. Catherine gave him one of her soft and decidedly indulgent smiles. Even with the wind blowing her strands of hair free from what she called a ponytail, she was a beautiful woman. Perhaps more so now than when he'd first met her.

"What?" she asked.

Gareth would have liked to tell her, but their guide said they should make sure they were securely in their seats. She wore that sly grin again and slid her arm through his. Suddenly the boat sped up, and his head rocked back. Alarmed, he grasped the metal handle before them.

The boat swerved to one side and then the other. The momentum pushed Catherine away from him, and he threw his arm around her to keep her at his side. She pressed her head into his neck. The boat straightened but the speed increased. What if it pitched over and they all ended up in the water?

Gareth cursed.

"I'm sorry," Catherine said, lifting her mouth to his ear. "After the Eye I should have warned you."

"You clever girl." So this was expected. Gareth grinned, thrilling now at the speed. When they slowed, he found himself disappointed that they finished the tour at a more leisurely pace.

"We *must* do this again," he said when they'd returned to the dock.

"I had to schedule that in advance." She laughed at his expression. "I'll check my schedule to see if I can get tickets on one of my days off. You can also see if Walter will bring you while I'm working."

"No. It must be with you." He lifted her from the boat. "You found it as exhilarating as I did."

"Yes." She looked up at him as he set her on her feet. "Now you know why I wanted to come."

"Indeed, I do." Gareth had to steel himself to keep from kissing her. A simple flirtation was fine, but he must take care not to mislead her or set himself up for possible hurt.

8

CATHERINE FOUND IT DIFFICULT TO sleep that night. Her day spent with the earl had left her unsettled, almost giddy. She hadn't felt that way since she'd first fallen in love. What a ridiculous thought. Good thing she wouldn't see him for a few days.

Gareth Hildebrand was turning out to be the most unique man she'd ever met. In some ways, he seemed almost an innocent, so oblivious to common, everyday things. Other times, it was obvious he was *no* innocent.

He also had a way about him that made him seem older than she understood him to be. It made her wonder what he'd lived through, what he'd lost. She hadn't bothered to ask him because he was bound to ask the same thing of her. Still, seeing how life had marked him left her curious.

The connection Catherine felt to him was another thing that troubled her. He was going back home. She couldn't allow herself to become attached to him only to watch him leave. It seemed like everyone in her life left, and she just didn't know if she had it in her to allow herself to care again.

Still, this had definitely been a better holiday so far than she'd anticipated. Catherine rolled over and gave a happy sigh. If she were to be honest with herself, it had turned into the best one she'd had in recent years. She thought he was enjoying their time together too.

At least, that was what she told herself, and she hoped she hadn't been misreading him. It didn't really matter. It was going to be difficult to go back to work, and she realized it was the first time in over a year that she wasn't looking forward to her job.

Against her will, Catherine's thoughts shifted back to that moment in the capsule when they'd held each other. Just thinking about it made her go hot all over again. Why had she ever thought that turning thirty would make her no longer vulnerable to feelings like this? Wasn't she too old to go all fluttery like a high-schooler? A quote one of her psychiatrist friends was fond of telling his clients came to Catherine's mind: denial was not a river in Egypt. She obviously wasn't too old for a man to make her pulse race.

She told herself again that it didn't matter. As attracted as she might be to Gareth, the man was leaving. The best she could do was to enjoy the little bit of time they had left. She knew she was not imagining mutual attraction, and she wasn't a complete fool to think he didn't see it too.

When the holiday month was over, she'd need to thank Aunt Nellie for asking her to play the guide. Since she'd first attended a Twickenham Manor ball, Aunt Nellie had shown nothing but support and sympathy. If she had suggested doing this a year ago, Catherine wouldn't have been ready. The timing had been perfect. The experience had brought her out of a gray funk that she'd lived in for too long. She felt alive.

Catherine glanced out her bedroom window. She was starting to enjoy life again.

"YOU SEEM DISTRACTED THIS EVENING, my Lord," Geoffrey said as he set out Gareth's pajamas.

"My mind is full," was all he could think to say.

How did he put into words what he was feeling after such a day? In that boat he'd felt so *alive*, thrills racing through him. It'd been unlike anything he'd experienced since he'd been a young man and had engaged in his first carriage race.

And that had paled to the feel of Catherine in his arms. He'd not expected her to do such a thing, in spite of all the casual touching the people in this time seemed to do. He'd seen enough people engaged in extremely amorous activities in public that he'd begun to accept it without thought.

But not from Catherine. He'd not been prepared for her to embrace him as she had. As he looked back on it, he wondered again if her allure had anything to do with the fae magic.

He examined Aunt Nellie's choice of words. Why would it be important for him to work *with* the magic? What did the magic expect from him?

His instincts told him it had to do with Catherine, that it was no mistake that she'd been asked to be his guide. Why? What would anything they might learn from each other have to do with magic? Was he discovering something here that was important for him in his own time?

Was it coming to care for this woman?

Gareth didn't trust his emotions. He'd allowed himself to assume that a simple declaration of his intent to court Reese would be enough to win her. But nothing he could have offered her would have been enough because he could not steal the love she already felt for another man.

And rightly so. What he'd felt for Reese had been admiration . . . and attraction. He would not deny that he'd felt that. However, over the years he'd been attracted to many women. Reese had been different. What he'd felt for her was more complicated. It was almost as though she had opened his mind to the possibility of something more, something such as he'd shared with Cecily. Something he might be interested in pursuing with Catherine.

Yes. Gareth had a few more weeks in this time. He wished very much to become even better acquainted with the doctor. More than would be possible in this visit to the future. Would she consider a holiday to the past? How would he know unless he risked his memories of Reese—and the possibility of reverting back to the man he'd been?

9

"THAT'S OUR RIDE," CATHERINE SAID and led Gareth to the tour bus that would take them on the all-day excursion to Leeds Castle, the Cliffs of Dover, and to Canterbury.

They'd done lots of these over the past couple of weeks. She'd had more fun than she could possibly have imagined when she'd found him lying on the floor of the portrait room that first evening. It seemed so long ago.

Her days were rich now, and it seemed like every waking moment was filled with thoughts of Gareth. What would he like to see next? What restaurant should she introduce him to? Even her coworkers had commented on how much happier she seemed. Her life would seem incredibly dull once he went back to his home.

"I must say," Gareth commented as he followed her aboard, "these large traveling carriages are much more comfortable than I would have imagined." He paused, as he did every time, and waited for her to take the window seat.

"Why do you do that?" she asked, sliding into it.

"Do what?" He sat beside her.

"Always give me the window seat? What if I got motion sick?"

That adorable crease appeared between his brows. She was getting fonder of it every day they spent together.

"Why, I take this position in case we are held up. I prefer to have myself between you and any possible assailant."

She probably should have been offended that he thought her incapable of defending herself. Instead, it made her think of her grandfather and tears burned in her eyes.

"Have I said something wrong, Catherine?" he asked, his brow furrowed with alarm.

"No, it's just something my grandfather would have done."

"Your grandfather was a gentleman then."

"Yes, an old-fashioned gentleman. He always took the position on the outside of the sidewalk for the same reason. I told a friend about it, and she said he was a chauvinist, but I thought it was loving and tender."

"And you miss him?"

"Yes," she said.

The tour guide started in on the explanation of their trip for the day and the two of them went quiet.

"I hope this is not too personal, but are you alone in the world?" Gareth asked when they were outside of the city and the guide had stopped pointing out things.

"I have people that I go out with sometimes. My life has been busy with work, and I haven't stayed in touch like I should have. That's something I may be ready to change." Since he'd talked with a lot of humor about his bossy nurse growing up, she asked, "What about you? Tell me more about your sister."

"I believe I've mentioned that she is much younger than I. Of late, we've become quite close. She comes of age soon, and I don't look forward to losing her." He glanced out the window but it didn't seem like he was taking in the scenery. "The only other relative worthy of mention is our fraternal grandfather's spinster sister. She's quite the character. When I was born, she said being called a great aunt sounded too old and didn't suit her at all."

"What did she want you to call her?" Catherine asked, wishing she could meet these two women.

"Grandmama." Gareth didn't quite roll his eyes.

"What did you call your grandmother?"

"She died when our father was young. Grandmama insisted since the title wasn't being used, that she could have it."

Catherine laughed. "She sounds a little like my American grandmother. Her family was originally from Germany, and she said to call her "Oma" because it sounded so much younger than grandmother. She was obsessed with looking young. She needn't have worried."

"What happened?" he asked.

"She went in for a facelift and had an allergic reaction to the anesthesia and died."

Gareth closed his eyes as though trying to decide something. Finally, he heaved out a breath and glanced at her.

"Would you please explain those words?"

"Oh, I'm sorry."

Sometimes Catherine thought she should just stop talking. She never knew which words would trip him up. He must have the strangest kind of amnesia because it didn't fit anything she knew of, and she'd asked at the hospital. She'd decided it might be psychological since what he could remember and what he couldn't seemed random, a selective kind of amnesia. Though that might not be fair since "selective" had the connotation that he had control over it.

"A facelift," she said, putting her palms to her cheeks and pressing the skin back toward her scalp, "is when they cut away sagging skin and pull it back to get rid of wrinkles. It makes people look younger."

Gareth opened his mouth and then let out a breath, considering. "Ah, yes, I can see that. Does it not give people a stretched appearance to their faces?"

"It can, depending upon how good the plastic surgeon is and how often they have it done." At his glazed look, Catherine added, "That's someone who performs that kind of operation."

"Yes." He nodded. "Grandmama has a friend who used arsenic wafers for her complexion. She made the mistake of leaving them out and her dog ate them."

Catherine gaped. "That's outrageous. Arsenic is a poison. What company is selling those? They should be reported."

"It was a long time ago," Gareth said quickly. "I don't believe one can purchase them anymore."

"I hope not. That kind of thing used to kill people." Catherine took a deep breath. "Tell me about your friends."

"I have many casual friends, but more political associates."

If he was involved politically, she wondered why she'd never heard of him before or recognized his face when she'd first seen the portrait.

"People you're close to?"

"No." His expression had turned thoughtful.

"I understand." Catherine held up her mobile. "We've never been more connected to each other yet we're still so far away. I'm sure you've seen how many people sit down in a restaurant and mess with their phones instead of talking to each other."

"Yes. I have found that strange."

"When we were in med school, we'd go out to eat after class and text each other while we were sitting at the table together. It was stupid. It can create a terrible kind of isolation, being surrounded by people and yet being alone."

"You have not done that while you've been with me," he said.

"No. I learned my lesson." Catherine glanced away, not wanting to talk about it.

"I apologize. I do not wish to pry," he said and was quiet for a few minutes. "What do you do with your time when you're not taking visitors to these sites?"

"I try to keep busy and have a purpose."

"To do good?" His voice had gone soft, and she looked at him.

"Who are you thinking of?" Catherine asked.

"How do you know that I'm thinking of someone?"

"You sometimes get a faraway look in your eyes. It makes me wonder who in your life puts it there."

"I find it a little disconcerting that you have learned to see that in me." His gaze moved to the window. "Aside from my sister, I'm not aware of any woman at home who would care to know me well enough to do that. Except, of course, those who would use it as a means to get access to my fortune."

"That's terrible." Catherine shifted in the seat, and he looked at her. She asked, "Do you really know women who are only interested in you for your money?" What woman couldn't see what a great guy he was?

"Either that or my title."

"Well, that's just stupid."

"Thank you, my dear." Gareth covered her hand with his, and the warmth of his touch sent the now-familiar jolt of attraction up her arm. He arched a brow, indicating that he'd felt it too, and the corner of his mouth quirked up.

"Ahead is Leeds Castle," the guide said, interrupting the moment. He pointed to a sign and went into an explanation of how the tour would go.

When they left the bus, Gareth offered her his arm. Catherine was more aware of him as she took it and listened quietly to the guide as they followed the group through the building. Gareth seemed especially fascinated with the information about the history of the house. She wondered if he couldn't remember it or had never visited it.

"Have you been here before?" he finally asked when they'd left the building.

"Yes, once when we first moved to England. My father had been here as a child and wanted to visit. It's so beautiful. I'm glad they've worked hard to preserve it."

Gareth paused for a moment to look out on the moat, and she wondered what he was thinking. His gaze landed on the gift shop, and he scowled.

"Is nothing sacred?" he growled.

"It's how they help pay to maintain the property. I'm happy to buy a few overpriced souvenirs if it means they can preserve this bit of history."

He gave a soft grunt, and she wasn't sure he was convinced.

They bought some sandwiches in the little shop nearby and boarded the bus again for Canterbury. Gareth was quiet but his gaze seemed to take in everything. Was this one of those places that he "sort of" remembered? Where she might have asked him about it, she decided it would be best not to.

After walking around Canterbury, Catherine was tired when they returned to the bus and began the trip back to London. Gareth continued to be introspective, and she found herself growing drowsy. When she started to nod off and her head gave a jerk, Gareth slipped an arm around her shoulders.

"Go ahead and rest, my dear."

She leaned against him, her eyes already closing. Her last thought as she drifted off was how good he smelled.

"Catherine," he whispered against her hair after what felt like only a few seconds, his cheek pressed against the top of her head. "We have returned to London."

"Wow." She straightened and yawned. "I can't usually sleep on a bus. Did you doze off too?"

"I did." He gave a soft, reflective smile as though he were pleased.

Walter was waiting at the terminal. Instead of Gareth offering her his arm, he took her hand. It felt good.

10

"I'D LIKE TO SUGGEST THAT we do something a little different today," Catherine said to Gareth at the end of their third week together. They were headed toward the pastry shop where the people now knew him by his first name. It seemed to please him whenever they called him Gareth.

"What would you have us do?"

"We're still doing the tour of Buckingham Palace to see the changing of the guard. What I'd to add is an event tonight. It's a fundraiser event for work, but it's at the Barbican Conservatory. We could take a tour during the day, but I thought it might be more fun for you to see how it can be used in different ways."

"A social function?" Gareth asked, perking up even more. "With your peers? How formal will the dress be? I wish to do you credit. Will I meet other female doctors?"

He was so adorable. Catherine had debated inviting him to be her plus-one. She hadn't gone last year because she couldn't bring herself to go alone. If she showed up with a guest this year, coworkers would assume he was her boyfriend and get way too excited for her. When he left next week, she'd have to deal with the pity thing again.

Last night, as she'd crawled into bed, she'd decided to go alone. Then she'd dreamed of saying goodbye to him at the end of his holiday here. A sense of dread had filled her, and this morning she still hadn't been able to shake it. Their time together was running out.

"Yes, you'll get to meet other female doctors. Do you want me to set you up with one of them?" Catherine had meant it as a joke and was surprised at the twinge of jealousy.

"Set me up?"

"Date someone." At his confused expression, she added, "It's when two people go to functions because they like each other romantically."

"Courtship? With someone *else*?"

Her heart did a little flip-flop. *Someone else.* The horror laced in his tone sent a thrill through Catherine that she had to push down. She had to admit she'd grown too fond of this handsome man with his charmingly old-fashioned manners, delight in the world around him, and even his gentle flirting.

"I was teasing you. I won't really set you up." Not likely. When he left, Gareth Hildebrand was going to leave a huge hole in Catherine's life. With so little time left together, she had no intention of sharing him with another woman.

"It's a formal reception, so you'll want to wear tails. If Aunt Nellie doesn't have anything for you, I'm sure we can find something."

"Will it only be doctors at this party?"

"Oh no. It's a fundraiser to help the families of children who have cancer and are going through long-term treatment. They come from all over the country and need someplace to stay while they're here. Lots of rich people and politicians are invited to the fundraiser. They get to rub shoulders in front of the press and show off how generous they are by making public donations."

Gareth frowned as he considered her. "I do not believe you wish to attend."

"Am I that obvious? Sorry."

They were at the pastry shop and ordered their food.

"Why must you attend if you do not wish to?" Gareth asked when they were heading to the Tube again.

"My boss wants everyone who's not working to make an appearance. Last year I volunteered to work that shift at the hospital so I didn't have to go."

"Something else is troubling you." Gareth was watching her closely again.

He didn't even question that it was. The man had an uncanny way of doing that, and it made Catherine think he could read her. She was usually able to keep her feelings hidden, something she'd had to learn to do for her job. How come he could see through her public face? Either she was getting sloppy and showing more than she intended, or Gareth was getting to know her well.

"I don't want people to misunderstand our relationship," she finally admitted.

He got that engaging grin of his. "You do not wish them to think I'm courting you."

There he went again, using those archaic terms. It was *so* him. There had to be something wrong with her that she found it attractive.

"Knock it off. You're way too full of yourself." She nudged his shoulder with hers, and he chuckled.

"It would be my honor to serve as your escort to this reception." Gareth took her hand, bowed, and kissed it.

Catherine's stomach went fluttery, warmth flowing from where his lips had touched her hand, up her arms, and into her core. For a second, she let herself imagine the two of them together, but she pushed the thought aside. Wishful thinking. Still, when Gareth Hildebrand returned to wherever he'd come from, she was going to miss him terribly.

GARETH WAS PLEASED to see Aunt Nellie leaving her office when he returned. She smiled and waited for him to reach her.

"It is good that I am finally able to speak with you," he said. "I have wondered if you were avoiding me."

"Simply busy, my Lord, I assure you. How are your sightseeing trips going?"

"I have been enjoying myself immensely. I must thank you for asking the good doctor to be my guide."

"I'm glad to hear it, my Lord. She sent me a text message about the reception. Top hat and tails, it is." Nellie indicated her office. "I must say that it is a good sign that she's invited you to meet her coworkers. Catherine's a close one."

Since there were servants in the hallways, Gareth waited until they had entered Aunt Nellie's office before speaking.

"Might I ask what happened to her? I can see in her eyes that she has suffered loss."

"That story is not mine to share, but I can say that she is alone in the world." She turned to face him. "Geoffrey will be here soon with some clothing options for you. Did Catherine say what color she would be wearing?"

"Black."

"Of course she is." Nellie sighed. "Someday that woman will wear color again."

Before he could ask what she'd meant, the door opened and several people entered, led by Gareth's valet. All carried several hangers with men's dress clothing. They lined up in a row, displaying the clothes.

"Now, my Lord, all we have to do is mix and match."

He watched, bemused, as she paced in front of the assemblage of clothing, glancing between him and a particular piece. Sometimes she'd shake her head and other times she'd nod. When she was finished, Aunt Nellie had selected a gray jacket, charcoal trousers, black waistcoat, a black and white-striped tie, and a light gray top hat.

"A white shirt and white handkerchief will set it off nicely, don't you think, my Lord?"

"I do," Gareth said, wondering about the black dress Catherine would be wearing. She'd said it was a formal event, but what the people here considered formal was so different from his own time. "I believe I would do the Ascot races justice wearing that."

"That, my Lord, is the idea." Aunt Nellie gave him one of her mischievous grins.

GARETH FOUND himself nervous as he sat in the car with Walter outside of Catherine's lodging. He'd thought himself beyond such a thing before a social gathering. Usually, he was bored.

"There she is, my Lord."

Gareth had the door open and was on the sidewalk before he'd taken the time to look. Catherine stood on the stoop, watching him, one brow arched appreciatively, a soft curve to her mouth.

She wore a full-length, close-fitting gown of black lace. The square-cut neckline and short sleeves softened the formalness without taking from its elegance. Catherine looked exquisite. An ache began in his chest, and he found it difficult to swallow. He removed his hat and bowed before putting it back on and making haste to the stairs to offer her a hand.

"My dear," he said, "there are no words."

Her cheeks flushed a becoming pink. "I would say the same thing about you except I *can* think of a word. *Hot.*"

"I don't—"

"It means she finds you attractive, my Lord," Walter said from where he stood holding the car's back door open for them.

"Stay out of it." Catherine smiled at the driver, taking the sting from the words. "But Gareth may need a protector tonight."

"Why?" He pulled her hand through his arm and guided her down the steps.

"Because the ladies will be after you, of course."

"The ladies are always after me."

"Ah. Poor baby," she said, her tone teasing. "What a poor fellow you are that the only reason any woman would want you is because of your title." Catherine rolled her eyes. "Not." She slid into the car.

Gareth stopped at the door and whispered to Walter, "Is it good to be *hot?*"

"Indeed, my Lord," the driver said, his tone serious. "It means you're the Pinkest of the Pinks."

"Did she mean it?"

"Most assuredly, my Lord. Have no fear of that."

Grinning, Gareth took the seat beside her.

"I meant to tell you how lovely you look tonight, Catherine."

"Thank you."

He met her gaze and found himself caught in it. While such a dress would have earned a carefully coiffed style in his day, there was something elegant in the way she had swept her long hair into a messy bun at the back of her neck.

A strand of hair had caught in her long earring, and Gareth reached over to gently pull it free. When his knuckle brushed against her cheek, her breath caught. The thrill caused his heart to thud hard.

She had beautifully-shaped lips, and he wondered what it would feel like to kiss them. He met her gaze. Seeing the same desire in them, he leaned closer. Catherine lifted her chin and her mouth opened a tiny bit. It was an invitation, and he meant to accept it.

Walter coughed, pulling Gareth back to his situation. The driver glanced at him through the mirror, shaking his head. It must not be appropriate. What an odd time it was. Gareth let out a deep breath, aware that Catherine was now sitting stiffly beside him.

He moved his hand so it was barely touching hers. When she

didn't pull it away, he shifted his so it covered hers. As she glanced at him, she turned her hand and laced their fingers. Perhaps it was just as well that they were not alone.

Walter pulled up to a curb and hopped out to open the door.

"We're not at the main entrance," Catherine said. "I wanted to point out a few things, so we'll walk."

"I will be nearby, as always, doctor." Walter shut the door.

When Gareth extended his arm, she shook her head and took his hand instead. It was the first time she had done so herself.

"The Cripplegate area was almost completely destroyed during the German Blitz," Catherine said as they walked between a complex of tall buildings.

"German Blitz?"

Catherine only hesitated a second before explaining. Her curious glance made him think she wished to ask more. Gareth imagined that were they to spend much more time together that she either wouldn't pause at all at his lapses.

"The Blitz was when the Germans dropped bombs on London from air planes in an attempt to destroy British industry and demoralize the people. London wasn't the only city hit, but about half of the forty thousand civilians who died were killed here." She looked at him grimly. "It didn't work. They were tougher than the Germans gave them credit for."

Every time Gareth learned more about the history between his time and this one, it drove home that this was no utopia. Catherine continued to talk about the construction of the complex of buildings. The architecture was very different from that of his time and not to his taste with its odd-shaped buildings.

"The Barbican Centre was built as an arts and learning center and includes all major art forms, like music, dance, theatre, and visual arts. Oh, and film too. That's all great to see, but I love the conservatory. Once we've made a showing at the reception, I'll take you there."

The event was a crush, and a large crowd waited outside.

When they finally reached the doors, she took something from her purse and handed it to a man. He nodded for them to enter.

Catherine took his arm then and walked quite close to him, scanning the people as though looking for someone. When she paused, Gareth put his mouth to her ear.

"Are you well, my dear?"

"I don't like crowds." Catherine shuddered, a faint sheen of sweat now on her forehead. She edged even closer to him. "Sorry. For some reason it's really bad tonight."

Gareth did the only thing he thought might help; he put his arm around her shoulders. As Catherine had done on the London Eye, she turned to face him and slid her arms around his waist. Her heart pounded hard against his chest, her breathing irregular. It reminded him of that first time in the Tube. Where he reacted poorly to heights, it was clear she did the same thing in a tight crowd.

She slowly relaxed and looked up at him. "Sorry. It's not usually this bad. There are just so many people in here."

"I don't mind." Gareth didn't attempt not to smirk.

"You, sir, are a terrible flirt." Catherine released him. "I hope I didn't wrinkle your coat."

"And who is your guest, Cathy?"

He didn't need Catherine's wince or the way she stiffened beside him to recognize the man for a predator. Gareth didn't like the way the man approaching them with a grin was looking at her. Gareth put his arm around her shoulders again and met the man's considering gaze.

"Oh, hello," she said, her tone one that Gareth had never heard her use before. "Gareth Hildebrand, may I introduce Doctor Boucher to you? He's one of the hospital's surgeons."

Catherine didn't extend her hand as she usually did when greeting people, so Gareth took his cue from her and didn't either. He quirked a brow and gave the man the bored glance and sniff that members of the Ton feared receiving from Gareth. It was the closest to a cut direct that people of this day would understand. When the doctor stiffened and his eyes narrowed, Gareth knew he'd hit his mark and quirked his mouth in the hint of a grin. The other doctor left in a huff.

"What has that man done to you, Catherine?"

"Not to me. He's just one of those creepy guys who thinks he's irresistible to women. He's always making sexually-loaded comments and talks about his prowess in bed. Very juvenile. He never *quite* crosses the line into a hostile work environment, but I can't stand him." Her gaze shifted. "Oh, there she is." Catherine took his hand and headed toward a small group of people.

Gareth allowed her to pull him along. This time she did shake their hands, so he offered his as well. He appreciated that while she didn't announce his rank, she honored it by how she introduced her supervisor and some coworkers to him. Catherine appeared to be comfortable as she chatted with them.

Bemused, he studied her. She conversed with others easily and appeared to have shaken her earlier fear of the crush. Then the press of people shifted as they always did. Her breath caught, and her grip tightened. Gareth put his arm across her shoulders, and she leaned against him. With him so close, her muscles relaxed. Finally, she excused them and turned to face him.

"Ready to see the conservatory?"

"Please."

Gareth offered her his arm, and she took it. When he covered her hand with his other one, she let out a sigh as though she appreciated his support.

"There's free champagne over there if you'd like some." She indicated a table with rows of filled flutes.

He glanced at the others in the room, the women drinking as freely as the men. "Would you like a glass?"

"I don't drink." Her tone had taken on an edge.

"Then I will not imbibe either."

She gave him a small smile. "This way. You're in for a real treat."

They were silent as they made their way through the crowded room. Only when they stepped into a nearly empty hallway did her hold on his arm ease.

"Sorry about that earlier." Catherine paused to let out a deep breath. "I don't know where that came from. I'm sometimes a little claustrophobic, but it's usually not something I can't handle."

"Clausto . . . what?"

"Claus*tro*phobic. It's a fear of small spaces or being closed in." She took his hand again. "This way."

"But you had no problem on the Eye."

"It wasn't that crowded, and I could see all around me. Sometimes riding the Tube can give me problems. When I was a little girl, before we moved to England, I was playing at a friend's house and hid in a chest. Her older brother thought it would be funny to lock me in. It took a while to find me, and I've had issues with tight spaces ever since."

"Yes, a memory like that would surely stay with you. As a boy I climbed too far up a tall tree on our property. I fell and broke my arm." He rubbed it in remembered pain. "My father was furious and said I could have killed myself."

"I wonder if that contributed to your fear of heights."

"Perhaps. I suppose I am fortunate that it had not manifested itself before the Eye."

They'd reached a door, and Gareth opened it. The sudden change in sounds and smells stole his breath away. Instead of the sterile concrete and tile of the hallways, he beheld a colorful expanse of glass walls, tropical plants and trees, and . . . the sounds of birds and running water.

"I know, right?" Catherine still held his arm and rested her cheek on his shoulder. "That's exactly how I felt the first time I came here."

"Where do the colors come from?" he asked.

"It's just colored lights. It adds to the exotic feel of the place. Come on."

After the chaos of the reception with its mass of people, the large conservatory with its three stories of hanging plants was an oasis. They walked slowly along the paths, passing several others who'd also sought refuge there. Gareth and Catherine spoke little as they strolled, enjoying instead the peacefulness.

"Did you like it?" she asked when they had returned to where they'd entered the conservatory. Catherine didn't look at him, instead glancing around the room. She wore a soft, satisfied smile.

"I did, and I thank you for allowing me to share this evening with you."

"No, Gareth." She looked at him then. "Thank you for coming. I don't know what I'd have done back there if I'd been alone. I owe you for that."

"I believe I already *owed* you, dear Catherine, after the Eye." He gave a quick bow of his head. "It was my pleasure to render my assistance to you. And any time you may have need of me." Gareth felt as well as heard the significance of his words, though he doubted the good doctor did.

"Have you seen enough?" she asked, her cheeks flushed enough that perhaps she had heard.

"Of the conservatory, yes." He brushed her cheek with his hand and turned toward the door.

CATHERINE STARED at the ceiling of her bedroom, unable to sleep. In spite of herself, she was getting much too attached to her old-fashioned gentleman. Part of her was glad that their time together was running out. He would go back home, and she would return to her life as it had been.

The thought left an ache in her chest. She didn't want to go back to picking up extra shifts to fill the emptiness. Her time with

Gareth had shown her that she was ready to do more. But what? Since she'd enjoyed the sightseeing she'd done with him, Catherine would like to explore further. She was close to paying off her school debt. Maybe when it was, she could save her money and holiday time for a single excursion each month.

Or maybe she could visit him.

11

"ARE WE FINISHED WITH MUSEUMS?" Gareth asked as he greeted Catherine at the end of their fourth week. He had planned to return to his time tonight after the Full Moon Ball, but as he had approached their final day together, he'd found himself wanting to extend his stay. He'd inquired of Aunt Nellie if he could remain longer, and she had been amenable.

"You didn't enjoy them?" Catherine glanced up from the brochure she'd been reading.

"I own that I'm not a connoisseur of art. I must also say that a few that you have taken me to have been quite disturbing." His stomach turned. "Why would anyone wish to celebrate such heinous acts as that fiend Jack the Ripper committed?"

"I'm sorry about that one," Catherine said, a little stiff. "I did think you enjoyed the Churchill War Rooms."

"Yes, I did. Quite fascinating."

But quite as unsettling in a different way. Gareth didn't know the words to express how troubling the concept of wars conducted on a worldwide scale had proven. It had been disturbing enough when she'd described the German Blitz but seeing pictures of the devastation had been chilling. Perhaps that had contributed to his dream of bombs falling from the sky that had wakened him in a sweat. It made him feel weak, and he didn't like to feel that way.

"I was thinking about getting tickets for the Harry Potter tour at Warner Brothers Studios this morning but decided you wouldn't enjoy that." She heaved out a breath, looking thoughtful. "We could see Windsor Castle." At his expression, she added, "Maybe not. I should have arranged for a day trip to Paris. I'd even have braved the underwater tunnel for you."

"*Underwater* tunnel?" Gareth asked weakly but held up a hand. "Don't explain. I believe I'd like to see Southwark Cathedral." At her surprised expression, he said, "You told me of its antiquity when we were on the Eye."

"Yes, I did, didn't I?" Her cheeks colored.

Gareth forced himself not to smile. She remembered that experience as well. He would most assuredly be staying another month.

"Is it far?" he asked.

"Not on the Tube." Catherine put the brochure into her purse. "It's close to the London Bridge, so you'll get a chance to see that too from the street."

"Very good."

Gareth extended his arm, and she took it. It felt right to have her at his side. Once again, he felt a powerful desire to show her his world. He fingered the metal tip of his cane, wondering if he could convince Aunt Nellie to tell Catherine about the time travel.

When they reached the cathedral, he found it was like many he'd visited over the years. Following the tour group through it, he tried to see it through Catherine's eyes. To him, it was simply an old church. When they finally approached a door to the outside, he couldn't help letting out a breath of relief.

"Meh?" she asked, her tone laced with humor.

"I beg pardon?"

"It means uninspiring." Catherine gave a soft sigh. "I'm sorry you didn't enjoy it."

Gareth came to an abrupt stop, tightening his hold on her.

"What is it?" she asked, alarmed.

"This," Gareth breathed. He pointed to a shining building in the distance that towered over everything in its proximity. "Catherine, you told me you most enjoyed the combination of the very old and the modern. Is this not the perfect example? We stand on the threshold of a building that has been in existence longer than your country, while we face this . . ."

"It's called the Shard, sometimes the Glass Shard. It's a relatively new office building. There are tours if you're interested." Catherine glanced up at him, a mischievous twinkle in her eyes.

Gareth chuckled and patted her hand. "I think I've experienced as much height as I care to. I find I'm satisfied admiring it from solid ground."

They stood quietly for a few minutes, their shoulders touching, in the shadow of the old and the new.

"Are you ready for some lunch?" she asked.

"Yes, I believe I am."

"What are you hungry for?" Catherine turned thoughtful. "There are a number of places to eat near Borough Market."

"A good inn will do."

"Okay. This way."

The route to the eating establishment proved a busy one, with a confusion of streets branching off. They found it necessary to walk under one of the above-ground, fast-paced motorways. He doubted he would ever adjust to those.

The noise did not lend itself to conversation, so they walked in silence. As he often did, Gareth wondered what she would think of his time. Except for her initial frustration with his errant comments, she had very pretty manners. With only a little instruction, he thought she would do quite well in society.

"This is it." Catherine pointed to a building on a rounded corner.

"*This* is the tavern?" He stared at the structure, having one of those odd experiences when he'd see a building that existed in his time but superimposed over what was before him with the changes of time. "It's a debtor's prison."

"It used to be." Catherine gave him another of her curious glances.

"Yes, indeed," Gareth said, quickly. "That's what I meant to say." He'd never been inside the building but had passed it once. It was now a tavern?

After the bright light outside, it took a few seconds for his eyes to adjust to the dimmer interior. There were no signs that it had ever been anything but an inn. If the expressions on the faces of the guests were any indication, the food was good. His stomach gave an embarrassing growl.

Fortunately, there was only one other couple waiting for a table. Gareth wished they were able to hire a private dining room.

"We timed it right," Catherine said as they were being seated at a small table near the entrance. She nodded toward the growing line of people. Because of the warmth of the day, all the outside tables were filled.

"When we're done, you can see the new London Bridge. That should give us plenty of time to return you to Nellie's so we can dress for the ball."

"Must we attend? I would much rather spend the time with you and not in a crush of people."

"You don't want to go?" She couldn't hide her disappointment.

"As long as I am in your company, I will be happy to attend." He opened his menu. "What do you recommend?"

They discussed their options and placed their orders.

"Why did you wish to study as a doctor?" Gareth asked when the maid had departed.

Catherine put her elbows on the table, rested her chin on her clasped hands, and studied him.

"Since this is your last day here," she finally said, "I think you owe *me* some answers. So, I'll answer your question if you'll answer mine first." The intensity of her gaze made him uneasy.

"I may not be at liberty to answer."

"Another cryptic comment." She leaned back in the seat, still watching him. "Let's give it a try. Where are you really from?"

"Lincolnshire." It was the truth, though he'd moved his house seat to Kellworth for its better proximity to London.

"They have modern conveniences there, so why are you so unfamiliar with things like this?" Catherine held up her mobile.

Gareth's heart thudded. He wanted so much to tell her.

"You said one question, my dear, and I answered it. Now you must answer mine. Why a doctor?"

"All right. I chose medicine partly because my grandfather was a doctor." She was watching him again with a gaze that seemed to see too much. "And partly because I watched my best friend die of leukemia."

Gareth hoped his ignorance about the word she'd used didn't show in his expression.

"See. Who doesn't know what leukemia is? It really is like you're a man out of sync with time." Catherine narrowed her eyes and shook a finger at him. "Maybe I should have asked *when* you're from."

Gareth's heart leapt into his throat, and he had to pinch his mouth closed. He needed to speak with Aunt Nellie.

He was about to stand, when a large, dark shape came smashing into the table outside, sending the people sitting at it flying.

It took a second before Gareth's mind had registered that one of the large carriages had crashed into the row of tables outside. The people inside the restaurant were screaming and scrambling away from the front of the restaurant.

"Not again," Catherine hissed and was in motion, running out the door toward the chaos.

Confused, he followed his instinct, grabbed his cane, and ran after her. Outside, cries and shouts to run overwhelmed his senses.

Catherine was kneeling by a prone figure who must have been struck by the carriage. Gareth stood frozen in place, staring at the pool of blood as bile rose in his throat. She pressed her fingers to the young man's throat and shook her head. After pushing the table aside, she knelt by a young woman and did the same thing.

"I don't understand what's happened," Gareth shouted over the screams.

"Terrorist attack, I think." Catherine helped the groggy young woman to sit up. "Can you stand?"

"What about—" the woman mumbled.

"We have to get you somewhere safe," Catherine said, her eyes darting around as if looking for additional danger.

Across the street, out of his range of vision, Gareth could hear more shrieks and the sound of people running. What else was happening?

"Gareth, I need you to get her inside to safety."

His heart racing, he rushed beside Catherine to assist the young woman to her feet. As soon as he had her, Catherine moved on to another person. The woman in his care was unsteady and stumbled when she tried to take a step.

Gareth dropped his cane and picked her up, his nerves on edge at the continued shouts in the distance. He reached the restaurant door but found it locked. He was about to give it a sharp kick, when someone opened it. The people inside had moved to a higher level and were huddled behind the wooden half-wall.

Their obvious fear brought Catherine's words into focus: *get her inside to safety*. Those cries must be from continued danger—and Catherine was still out there.

"Help her," he commanded as he put the woman into the arms of the man who'd opened the door. Gareth turned to leave.

"Stay inside," a woman called, holding one of the mobile devices.

"I must help—"

"But *look*!" She pointed outside.

A man was striding across the street toward the restaurant. His head was covered by the same odd headscarf, with holes for the mouth and eyes, that had been worn by the driver of the carriage. Was it the same man come to render aid?

Then sunlight reflected on something in his hand. A large knife.

Catherine.

Gareth bolted out the door, the muscles in his shoulders tight. At first he couldn't see her. Where had she gone?

Movement to the right showed her in a small space between the building and the crushed carriage. She knelt by a man, her jacket pressed against his head. There was only one way out, toward the madman.

Between Gareth and Catherine, near an overturned table, lay his abandoned cane. He lunged for it. Spinning around, he faced the attacker as he came around the carriage. Gareth saw death in the lunatic's eyes. They darted to where Catherine knelt.

"*No*," Gareth growled and stepped between them.

With a roar, the man raised the knife and launched himself toward Gareth. He raised his cane reflexively in a fencing parry to block the blow. It deflected the large knife from driving into his neck. The attacker jumped back, still gripping the blade. Gareth shifted the cane and now held the weighted end toward the attacker.

The man lunged again. Catherine screamed a warning, but Gareth was already in motion. Skipping back, he parried the blow but slipped on the blood. His stagger moved him out of the way of a direct hit. It grazed him, sending hot pain up his left arm. The attacker moved as though to come at Gareth again. He tensed but at the last second the man feinted toward Catherine.

Swinging the cane low, he struck the man's knee with a sharp blow from the side. He fell, and Gareth brought the cane down on the madman's head. The knife skittered to the ground. Gareth kicked it out of reach. The attacker lay still.

His hands shaking, Gareth was about to turn to Catherine when another man moved into view.

"Put down your weapon," the man in a black uniform shouted harshly.

Gareth stiffened.

"He's talking about your cane," Catherine said, still pressing her jacket against her patient's head. "He's with the police. Do what he says."

Gareth dropped his cane.

"Hands on your head," the man growled.

"Do it, Gareth," Catherine hissed when he hesitated.

Confused, he slowly did as he'd been told. Another man started patting his clothes. Gareth met Catherine's gaze, his brows raised. Had he not just brought down the assailant?

"I'm an A&E doctor," Catherine called. "I've got a severe scalp wound here with arterial bleeding. He's lost a lot of blood. I don't know what else."

The policeman said something into a device on his shoulder. "I have someone coming." He glared at Gareth. "You stay against the wall." He then moved on.

"They don't know who to trust so just cooperate," Catherine said.

Gareth nodded, numb and confused, his body shaking with the aftermath of it all. Perhaps it made some kind of sense in this day gone mad. Something warm trickled down his arm. The reminder was followed by a stab of pain. He glanced at the dark sleeve of his jumper. There was a slice in the fabric, the area around it moist with his blood.

Others wearing uniforms now swarmed around them. One dropped to her knees beside Catherine, who went into a description of the injuries.

"I have this now," the policewoman said. "You can go be with your friend. They'll want to question you both."

Catherine came to stand beside him. She looked a mess, covered in blood, her eyes glistening. Gareth held out his arms, and she stepped into his embrace.

"I don't understand what happened," Gareth said again, his voice soft.

"No one understands terrorists." At his blank expression, she added, "It's someone who uses random violence, especially against civilians, for fear and intimidation, usually for political purposes."

They held each other until a man in uniform came up to them.

"Do you have ID?" the policeman asked.

"It's in the restaurant," Catherine said. "We were in there when it happened."

The door to the tavern opened, and the woman who'd told Gareth to stay inside, stepped out.

"This man stopped that nutter," she cried, holding up her phone. "I got it all on my mobile." When the policeman reached for it, she pulled back her hand. "I've already uploaded it online."

While they argued, a woman wearing a medical vest approached Gareth and Catherine. She pointed at him.

"Is that your blood?"

Catherine shook her head, but Gareth nodded.

"*What?*" She stepped back. "Did he stab you?"

Gareth pulled back the sleeve of his jumper and exposed a slash on his arm. Catherine then said a word that no lady of quality should know, much less repeat, and peered at his arm.

"You should have told me you were hurt."

"My Lord," Walter's familiar voice called from nearby.

The driver made a subtle movement with his hands and a blowing motion. Gareth thought he saw powder float onto the female medical person. She immediately moved to the officer who was arguing with the woman from the restaurant. Others from inside had joined. Then Walter made the blowing motion again, and the powder rested on Gareth and Catherine.

"This way, my Lord, doctor," the driver said.

"Stay with me, my dear." Gareth took Catherine's hand. She blinked, her expression slightly dazed.

Without any effort, Walter was able to guide them through the chaos. Once they were inside the car, he sped off, once again able to navigate the congested street with ease. Only when they were clear did he pull over and turn around.

"I need each of you to take a sip of this," the driver handed over a small bottle, "and then I must see to that arm, my Lord."

Gareth took a drink and handed the rest to Catherine. As she sipped the remaining tasteless liquid, he held up his arm. Walter smoothed an ointment of some kind over the cut. It burned at first, then tingled.

"One more thing, my Lord." He poked his arm with something that stung like a pin prick before turning around. "Penicillin for infection and tetanus." Walter then drove them away.

Gareth's arm itched. Drowsily, he pulled back his sleeve. The cut had closed and was now a pink scar. He put his uninjured arm around Catherine's shoulder, and she leaned into him. His eyelids grew heavy, and he closed his eyes.

CATHERINE STARED at the rearview mirror, waiting for Walter to glance back at her. He often did that when he was driving them places. This afternoon, though, he seemed determined not to.

She reached over and picked up Gareth's limp arm, brushing her thumb over the new scar. Whatever the driver had put on it must have a residue because her thumb tingled a little. How was it possible to heal a cut so quickly?

The aftereffects of the attack should have left Catherine shaking, yet ever since Walter had given her that liquid to drink, she'd been quite calm. She felt emotionally removed from what had happened, but she still had questions. Like, what drug had Walter used on them? Where did he come off giving people shots of penicillin and tetanus? Yet she couldn't bring herself to get fussed about it.

Catherine ran her thumb over the new tissue again. She must be suffering some kind of post-traumatic response, though she'd thought her experience in the A&E would have saved her from that. Apparently not.

She gently set Gareth's hand back down on his leg and straightened so she could watch his sleeping face. He'd stood between her and that terrorist. Gareth could have *died*. Catherine's heart pressed into her throat, making it hard to swallow. Somehow, the image of him defending a woman's honor while dressed in old-fashioned clothing fit him.

A lock of his dark hair had fallen out of place, and she brushed it aside. He was usually so fastidious about his appearance. She wondered for a second what it would be like to see him awake first thing in the morning with his hair mussed from sleep and the beginning scruff of a beard. An exquisite kind of tenderness for him started in her chest and spread through her body.

Catherine pulled back her hand. There was no point in going there. He was leaving tomorrow, and she'd never see him again. Why had Aunt Nellie insisted that Catherine be his guide? Hadn't she already lived through enough heartache, enough loss?

She shifted in the seat, so she was positioned to watch both men.

"What did you do, Walter?" she asked.

"Aunt Nellie will explain."

Catherine examined her hands for cuts. It would somehow be a fitting end to this horrific day to get a bloodborne disease because she'd treated the man without gloves. Had he survived? It was too late to have done anything differently, and she knew she wouldn't have.

"I want to go home," she said.

"Aunt Nellie will know when that is best."

Catherine heaved out a breath. She felt too calm, too emotionally removed from what had happened. It was almost as though she'd been given a tranquilizer. All she wanted was to go home so she could shower and change her clothes. She glanced at her shirt. It and her jeans were also stained. The outfit was a loss, including her jacket, which was still outside the restaurant.

"Oh, Walter," she said, leaning forward, "I left my purse in the restaurant."

"I'll have someone retrieve it for you. Have no fear." He still hadn't looked at her.

Catherine watched his face in the mirror again. She could almost see the hair on the back of his neck standing on end, so he must be aware of her scrutiny.

"Will you tell me what you did back there with the powder?" she asked.

His eyes darted to the mirror, but he averted them again.

"I can't say."

So, he wasn't supposed to tell her. Then why had he put the medicine on Gareth's arm in front of her? It was almost as though he'd given her a clue on purpose.

Catherine leaned her head against the seat, took Gareth's hand in hers, and laced their fingers. Her mind drifted back to the attack. He could have been killed today. They were both lucky to be alive. He hadn't hesitated to run after her to help. Had he really been clueless about what was going on? If he'd understood what was happening, would that knowledge have kept him inside? Her instincts told her he would still have come to help.

What man, at his age, could have lived in a world that didn't know what terrorism was? It was impossible. Catherine started.

As impossible as an ointment which could almost instantly heal a cut that should have required stitches?

The impression came to her again that Gareth Hildebrand was a man out of time. That was ridiculous, though. People couldn't travel through time. Even if she believed in such a thing, it was impossible. She'd read a few time travel novels, and they never made sense to her. If someone were really able to travel through time, they'd end up floating in space because the earth would have moved. If one traveled from one place to another—

Catherine broke off the thought, almost laughing. She'd used one of Gareth's old-fashioned terms. Old-fashioned. Travel through time. It was impossible. But, so was a magical healing cream. Her thoughts were going in circles, which was getting her nowhere.

Catherine brought Gareth's hand to her cheek. She could have lost him today. Her heart twisted, her eyes burning. She was growing way too attached to him. How had she let this happen? He was going to leave and break her heart.

She glanced up at the rearview mirror and found Walter watching her. He dropped his gaze. Only then did she pay attention to their surroundings and realized they weren't heading back to her flat.

"Where are you taking us?" she asked.

"Twickenham."

"I don't want to scare your guests." She indicated her hands and clothing.

"Aunt Nellie has staff awaiting our arrival. I'll drop you both off at the servants' entrance."

"All right." Catherine didn't have the energy to argue.

Drowsy, she rested her head on Gareth's shoulder. He wrapped his arm around her again and shifted so their bodies nestled together. His closeness filled her with comfort, and she wondered how her heart could swell and ache at the same time.

12

WHEN THE CAR PULLED UP to Twickenham Manor, Gareth roused. He thought he must have been dreaming, but he couldn't remember of what.

Catherine must also have fallen asleep, and he was loath to wake her. He liked the feel of her resting against his chest. She usually smelled good, but now there was an odd metallic tang to her fragrance.

Walter turned off the engine, and Gareth knew he must wake her. He realized then that she held his hand, their fingers entwined. The smattering of blood made the memory of what had happened come rushing back to him.

That maniac had been trying to kill *her*. Gareth's body began to shake, and it took all his strength to fight it.

"Catherine," he whispered. "We've arrived."

She stirred and would have pulled back her hand, but he tightened his grip. He sensed that the events of that day had pushed their relationship over the mountain that had previously blocked them. He didn't wish for this greater sense of intimacy to disappear. He knew in his gut that if he allowed her to pull back again, she would.

"Are you well?" he asked.

"I'm alive. We're both alive," Catherine whispered, her eyes blinking rapidly against the sudden moisture there, "which is more than I can say for some of those people."

"You were amazing." Gareth gave his admiration of this woman full rein. "I know many men who would not have rushed into danger as you did today."

"And I know many women and men who would have."

"Doctors you know?" When she gave him a wan smile, he said, "Then the doctors of today are made of sturdier stuff than I normally see."

"I beg pardon, my Lord," Walter said. "Aunt Nellie has arranged for her guests to be engaged in activities at this time, but we must get you both inside before they return." He exited the car and opened Gareth's door.

He slid out but continued to hold firmly to Catherine's hand, gently urging her to exit with him. As he watched her straighten, an image of her kneeling beside the poor victim, holding her jacket against his head in an effort to save his life, appeared to him. It struck Gareth again how vulnerable she'd been there, unable to defend herself. He pulled her into his arms.

"I was afraid the man would kill you," he whispered into her hair, his voice gruff.

"I thought he was going to kill *you*."

Catherine met his gaze, and that warmth he'd felt on the Eye hit him again, stronger than before. Gareth had wanted to kiss her then, but he'd hesitated. What if she had died today? He leaned closer, and she lifted her chin.

"Beg pardon, my Lord," Walter said with a sense of urgency. "We must get you both out of sight."

"I will be patient," Gareth said, still holding her gaze, the feel of her heart pounding a matching rhythm to his own. "Shall we go in?"

She nodded, and he released her. Keeping their clasped hands against his chest, he turned. They followed the driver into the house, where Nellie was waiting with a number of her staff members.

"What a dreadful experience you've had," she said, her expression sad. "We must get you both cleaned up. Catherine, I recommend that you stay the night with us. Doctor or not, after what you've been through, I don't like the idea of you going back to your flat alone."

Gareth glanced at her, not sure Catherine would accept the offer, but she didn't argue. They walked in silence until they reached his room. He hated having to release her and brought their clasped hands to his cheek.

"It won't be long, dear Catherine," he assured her.

"You promise?"

"On my honor." Gareth brought their stained hands to his lips to kiss her knuckles, but she stopped him.

"Bloodborne diseases," she whispered.

Recalling Reese's comments about blood, Gareth accepted the caution and released her hand. He bowed and turned to enter his room. Geoffrey stood waiting for him, his expression one of sympathy.

"You made a grand showing, my Lord."

"How would you know this?"

"Several people must have been recording everything on their mobiles from the safety of the tavern. It's all over the internet.

"Aunt Nellie may show it to you later, my Lord." Geoffrey pointed to the bathing room. "I would recommend a shower first. Once you're clean, you might enjoy a good soak."

When Gareth was finally able to sit in the hot water, he breathed a sigh of relief, the tension in his taut muscles easing.

Whatever Walter had dusted them with must have faded. Memories of the day began to flood Gareth's mind. Catherine could have died today.

He'd already accepted that he hadn't been in love with Reese and that what she'd done was put cracks in the walls he'd built around his heart. Catherine had laid waste to them and exposed his vulnerability.

For the first time since Cecily and their son had died, Gareth allowed himself to cry.

13

GARETH ENTERED AUNT NELLIE'S PARLOR, where he found her sitting at a table set for tea. He'd last eaten at breakfast, and it seemed an eternity since he and Catherine had shared those pastries. He bowed to his hostess and kissed her hand.

"I will wait to pour until Catherine joins us, my Lord." Aunt Nellie signaled for him to sit. "To use a rather outdated expression, you look a little worse for wear."

"I feel it." Gareth took a seat, missing for the first time in days the familiarity of his old way of dress. He feared that his memory of jeans and polo shirts would be forever tainted with the blood of innocents.

"I must apologize for your unfortunate exposure to this scourge of modern life, my Lord. It was a horrific experience." Nellie sighed, her expression sad. "I fear this is something the people of this time must live with. It was not only fortunate that you both escaped alive and intact, but that so few people were killed or injured."

"So *few*?" Gareth stared at her.

"I'm afraid there have been too many such incidents where even more people were killed or injured, some of them children."

"And I had thought to experience paradise." Gareth gave a bitter chuckle, his voice rough with emotion again. He'd not before considered himself a man of sensibilities, but perhaps that was untrue.

"I have lived a very long time, my Lord, and I have found that no time is perfect. There is good and there is bad in all ages. What becomes important is what people choose to do within their sphere of influence."

"You sound like Reese."

"Perhaps." Aunt Nellie wore a soft smile. "She's headstrong and sometimes unreasonable, but there are certainly worse comparisons."

"I have come to understand her passion to make the world a better place." Gareth rested one foot on the rung of his chair and clasped his raised knee. "I'm happy that she had such an influence on my sister." He added, more softly, "And on myself."

"What are your plans now, my Lord?" Aunt Nellie asked.

Gareth considered her question. While he'd planned to stay another month, he no longer wished to gad about the city. He had an uncomfortable feeling that he might embarrass himself by jumping at sounds and be always looking over his shoulder.

"Whatever you decide, I would advise you not to go on anymore excursions, my Lord," Aunt Nellie said, as though she'd read his thoughts. "Once Catherine joins us, I believe I should share with you both what is all over the internet. The video has gone viral, to use a modern expression, and the news stations have picked it up."

"Walter mentioned this viral thing, but I didn't understand."

"Let me explain, my Lord. I believe you're familiar with the pictures Catherine can take with her mobile, as I'm sure she's taken some of the two of you. Is that correct?"

"Yes, she has."

"Those same mobiles have the ability to record moving pictures, my Lord, often referred to as videos. Modern technology allows them to be put in places where others can see them quickly —the internet." Aunt Nellie gave him a kind smile. "I'm afraid that's what happened, and you are now famous."

Gareth leaned back in his chair, uneasy. What would it mean in this time to be famous?

"I don't like the sound of that."

"It's not good in this day for a man to have no personal identification, my Lord."

"The police officer was asking for that when Walter arrived."

The door opened, and they both turned to face Catherine, who watched them anxiously. She also looked the worse for wear. Gareth leapt to his feet and went to her. With a warm and grateful smile, she took the hand he offered. He threaded their fingers and pressed their joined hands to his chest.

"How are you feeling?" he asked.

"Not very rested, if that's what you mean." Catherine looked at Nellie. "Was someone able to retrieve my purse?"

"Yes. Please, sit." Their hostess indicated a sofa near the tea table. After they were seated close together, Nellie reached to the side of her chair and pulled out a purse.

"Thank you." Catherine took it and set it at her feet. "I don't understand how Walter was able to get us away from there. I expected the police to stop us."

Gareth exchanged a knowing glance with Aunt Nellie, one not lost on Catherine. She heaved out a deep, impatient breath.

"Please don't put me off, Aunt Nellie," she said. "I may not know exactly what's going on, but I know *something* is. Besides whatever it was Walter did, Gareth doesn't fit here, not in this century, and I'd even say he doesn't fit in the one before that."

"I've anticipated you might." Aunt Nellie gave him an understanding glance. "Not that I blame you, my Lord. I can trust that, because your memories are intact, you haven't breached our agreement."

"You're talking in riddles," Catherine said, exasperated. "Please just tell me what's really going on."

Smiling faintly, Aunt Nellie launched into the same explanation she'd given him.

"Ley lines? You're a faerie and *magic* brought Gareth to his future?"

"Yes," Aunt Nellie said, simply.

At Catherine's flat look, Gareth chuckled. She frowned at him.

"Are you making fun of me?" She tried to take back her hand, but he tightened his grip and pressed it to his lips.

"Of course not." He held up his arm to show her the new scar. "I don't mock you; I *sympathize* with you. Two months ago, I was faced with a similar situation where I was presented with actions and words that made no sense. I reached the conclusion that the people I'd met," he had to look down, "and come to care about were not from my time, that their words and behavior were not odd simply because they were Americans." He glanced up and met Catherine's gaze, making his expression as open as he could, with no dissembling. "I came to Aunt Nellie and insisted that she allow me to see this future. She agreed."

Catherine sat in silence, thoughtful.

"When are you from?" she finally asked, and her tone of belief warmed his heart.

"When I left, it was 1850."

"So his portrait really is from then." She glanced at Nellie, who nodded. Catherine asked, "What's with the picture anyway? It *feels* important."

"It *is* important. As I mentioned, the magic can cause people to travel accidentally, but if I paint a special portrait of that person to act as an anchor, they can travel to any time where the painting is in existence. His Lordship chose to travel to the same time his friends had come from."

Gareth was grateful for her discretion. He didn't understand why it was important that Catherine not know of his initial fascination with another woman. Not yet. What he felt for the doctor was so much stronger than his initial attraction to Reese. He would always be grateful that she'd forced him to see the world in a different light, to feel again. To hope again.

Gareth knew now that Catherine was that hope.

SHE SAT QUIETLY while Aunt Nellie poured tea and asked innocuous questions about whether or not Gareth wanted sugar or what he'd like to eat. Too much had happened, and Catherine couldn't process everything.

She felt like her emotions were in the eye of a storm. She'd just come from a traumatic experience, and she hadn't felt the full backlash yet. Then Nellie's little story had shifted the day from horrific to a faerie tale.

Catherine looked at her hand joined with Gareth's. A man out of time. Her curiosity itch had been well and truly justified. Faeries and magic. There had definitely been something going on at Twickenham Manor. If she woke, would she find that none of it had happened, that those people outside the restaurant would still be alive, well and whole?

That Gareth wasn't real?

She held his hand tighter, like if she could keep it there it wouldn't be a dream. When Nellie had offered him his cup of tea, he'd taken it with his left hand and kept his right in Catherine's. She was glad. At least in this moment, he was real.

"My dear, I am almost sorry you've been brought into this, but I believe it is no accident." Aunt Nellie nudged Catherine's hand with a cup, and she accepted it. Nellie continued, "I have added a touch of tonic to your tea, which will make you feel much better."

"One of *those* tonics?" Gareth asked, a hint of humor now in his voice.

How could he think any of this was funny? Then Catherine remembered the first time she'd seen him, kneeling on the floor and looking about to be ill. Nellie had given him something to drink that had put him right.

Catherine took a tentative sip of the tea, and a warmth beyond that of the liquid flowed down her throat and spread throughout her body. The unsettled feeling she'd been fighting faded. She took another sip, and it didn't seem to matter anymore that Gareth had been born nearly two hundred years ago. When he'd been born, it was only a few years after the War of 1812. What an odd thought.

"Does the time travel always make people ill or is it like motion sickness and only some people experience it?" Catherine finally asked.

"Everyone has a slightly different experience." Aunt Nellie offered a small plate of macaroons, but Catherine shook her head, still sipping her tea and refusing to let go of Gareth. Nellie gave an understanding smile and continued, "Some people experience nausea as his Lordship did, others may simply have some dizziness, but everyone feels at least a small amount of pain. I suppose how much depends upon what their threshold is."

"Will I respond the same way when I return home?" Gareth asked, blanching.

Hearing him say it drove a sharp pain through Catherine's heart. Returning to 1850 would be even worse than she'd feared. At least in a modern time they could have arranged to meet again. She might have visited him. He could have shown her his home that he talked about so lovingly. They'd have the time to get to know each other better.

Only now did she realize how much she'd clung to the possibility that, if they wished for it, they could see each other again, that this could be the start of something. Now she knew the truth: Gareth Hildebrand would be going back to a place where she couldn't reach him. The disappointment almost crushed her.

"What is it?" he asked.

"I won't be able to see you again," she said, her voice soft. "When you leave, we'll say goodbye forever."

"I don't wish to say goodbye to you, Catherine."

"But you'll be going back to 1850."

"Come with me." Gareth shifted in the seat and faced her, his expression pleading. "I came to your time, expecting a utopia. Mine isn't one either, but there is a beauty and grace in it nonetheless. Let me show you *my* world."

Catherine swallowed. She knew her history. Women hadn't been treated well in his time. If he'd been so disbelieving about her being a doctor, how would others act? She started to shake her head. He brought her clasped hands to his lips and kissed her knuckles, making her stomach twist.

"Come for a visit, Catherine," he said. "I wish to introduce you to my sister Ellen."

"Before you decide," Nellie interrupted, "I believe I should show you a viral video of today's incident."

She rose and retrieved a laptop from a table. It woke at her touch and showed a video already paused. It'd been taken from the window inside the tavern and apparently started not long after Catherine had run outside because Gareth was following her out the door. Her stomach turned as she watched herself moving from victim to victim. While she'd been in the midst of it, she hadn't noticed the screaming.

She went a little numb when the terrorist strode into view. He'd definitely been coming for her. Simply because she'd been there or because she'd been helping the injured? Then Gareth had gone into action with his cane. Aunt Nellie stopped the video.

"Everyone is asking about the mysterious man who stopped

the terrorist with a cane," she said. "However, they know the identity of the doctor who rushed outside to render aid."

"How?" Catherine gasped, her gaze snapping to Nellie's.

"I would assume because someone from your work recognized you and notified the authorities. Many people are also questioning why the police allowed the two of you to leave with an 'unidentified' man. Walter was wise enough to keep his face away from the cameras. He also had the foresight to muddy up the license plate. We'll need to keep that particular vehicle out of use for a while."

"They can't interview Gareth." Catherine reached for her purse. "What am I going to tell them?"

"I would completely understand if you didn't wish to be subjected to police interrogation or press interviews in your current state," Aunt Nellie said with her usual calm. "You have the option to take a few days to mend emotionally. I suggest you return with his Lordship to 1850."

Beside her, Gareth's hand had twitched. Catherine glanced at him and found him attempting to school his features. She reached up and stroked his cheek, wishing she could do more. That would have to wait until they didn't have an audience.

"Return with me, Catherine," he whispered, his voice full of pain. He was as troubled by the day's events as she was.

She wished she weren't so tired or the tea hadn't muted her feelings so much. She needed to make a logical decision. Though, maybe the tea was a good thing since it removed the emotional element from the decision. Once she had time to pull herself together, she thought she could deal with the aftermath here while protecting Gareth's identity. She faced Nellie.

"I don't want to get in anymore trouble with the authorities. If I disappear for a few days, it could be a major problem, and I might lose my job."

"When you return, it will be as though you've not been gone. As you've spent the past month showing his Lordship this time, he can spend the next month showing you his. Together you can try to forget the dreadful experience you've both lived through." Aunt Nellie met her gaze with kindness. "The one thing I can offer you is *time*."

"How will I get there?" Catherine asked. "You mentioned needing a painting for an anchor, but I don't have one in his time."

"His Lordship does have one, so you would travel with him."

"What if I wanted to make a return visit to see him again, but he's not here to take me?"

"You can take the portrait I painted of you along. It will then be in both times."

"I like this suggestion." Gareth's hand tightened over hers again. "I have no wish to bully you to agree but neither do I wish to say farewell."

Catherine's mind went through her options again. She really didn't want to talk to the police yet. The most appealing decision was to go with Gareth.

"You will be able to stay with him as long as you need," Aunt Nellie said with a twinkle in her eyes, "with no one in this time any the wiser."

"Should I not return with her to this time to speak with these authorities?" Gareth asked. "No gentlemen would abandon a lady in a difficult situation."

"I don't know if that would be wise, my Lord. In a perfect world we would be able to make the video disappear, but sometimes things happen that are outside of our control and ability to fix. It might be best if you simply disappeared. Catherine can say you left town but that she has no way to reach you. She wouldn't even have to perjure herself."

"I brought him with me to a work party and introduced him to some of my coworkers," Catherine said. "If they recognized me from that video, they're bound to remember him."

"If you return with his Lordship, you'll have time to come up with an explanation."

"Will you come with me?" Gareth asked, his tone now excited.

Catherine's stomach knotted at the same time her pulse quickened. She could visit the past and see Gareth's home. She wanted to do this, to get away from this nightmare. Most importantly, she wouldn't have to say goodbye yet.

"I'll do it," she said.

14

GARETH WAITED IMPATIENTLY FOR AUNT Nellie to assist Catherine to dress for the journey. In spite of the weight of what had happened, he now also felt a sense of lightheartedness. He hadn't experienced it since he'd been a youth, before life had dealt him so many blows.

Donning again the clothing he'd worn when he'd left his own time had driven home how he'd changed in these few weeks. He felt disconnected from the man who'd departed from 1850 Twickenham. As anxious as he'd been to come, he was ready to be gone from this future.

Gareth started pacing the room. After nearly dying today, he wanted—*needed*—to see Ellen and verify her safety. He wanted to know that she was happy.

Now that he knew how intelligent and capable women could truly be, he understood that he had done his sister a grave disservice. When she'd left finishing school, she'd somewhat wistfully expressed a desire to continue her education. He hadn't taken her comment seriously, and she'd not mentioned it again. If she were offered the opportunity, what would she study?

A knot of fear twisted his gut. Was the only place she could seek such an education in the future—where there were terrorists? What kind of bargain would that be, to allow his sister the freedom to choose a destiny that could result in hers being a crumpled body lying dead at the hands of a madman? Could Ellen attend a university near Reese?

Reese. Gareth paused in his pacing. He'd fooled himself with her, allowing himself to believe that after three day's acquaintance he wanted to court her. Would he have found after a longer acquaintance that his resolve would have strengthened or discovered that they did not suit? It was of no consequence. He hoped that she thought of him now as he did her, as a friend. With Reese, that was sufficient. With Catherine, it was not.

At the sound of voices outside the door, Gareth turned to face it, straightening his jacket. It opened and Catherine stepped in, dressed—not in the pale blue shimmery confection she'd worn when he'd first seen her—but in a dark pink gown fit for a lady of quality in his day. He thought the color would be quite fetching on her when the hollowness to her eyes had gone. Gareth bowed.

Catherine curtsied and lifted her hand. He took it and pressed it to his lips. His mind went back to when she'd cupped his face. For a second, he'd thought she meant to kiss him. It had left him so surprised that he'd failed to take advantage of it. That was twice now, and he regretted the lost moments. Had he kept his wits, he'd have taken her in his arms and shown her how much she meant to him, regardless of their audience. Now, he must be patient.

"Here is your painting, Catherine," Aunt Nellie said. "When you arrive, instruct me to place yours next to his Lordship's. It will then be an anchor for you in both times."

Gareth glanced at Catherine, and they moved toward his painting.

"You must be touching," Aunt Nellie said, tapping her chin with a finger. "I believe if the good doctor will put her arms around your waist that it will free your hands to carry the portrait."

Catherine stepped up to him and slid her arms, not just around his waist, but around his waist *inside* his coat.

"One must remember the time one is going to, Catherine," Nellie chided.

Grinning, Catherine moved her arms to the outside of his jacket and rested her cheek against his shoulder. Gareth brought his arms around her, and Aunt Nellie placed the painting in his hands.

"Some travelers have told me that if you close your eyes, it's less unsettling to your stomach. Others say it only makes it worse. I will let you decide." Aunt Nellie patted Catherine on the arm. "I hope you have an enjoyable stay."

"Can we take the tea before to help?" Catherine asked.

"We have tried that," Aunt Nellie said. "It doesn't help."

Catherine took a deep breath against him. It reminded him of that day not long ago on the London Eye.

As Aunt Nellie swirled her hands, Gareth began to speak softly.

"Kellworth has beautiful gardens. My sister, Ellen, has a fascination for horticulture and oversees them. She spends her winters searching seed catalogues for the next year. She has quite an eye for design—"

The sickening dizziness hit him, and Gareth broke off. As he felt the sensation of falling, Catherine must have also, for she gasped and held him closer. He tightened his arms around her, trying not to jab her with the edges of her portrait. Nausea hit him, and he clenched his teeth against the too-familiar taste of bile.

"Did you mean to bring someone with you, my Lord?" Aunt Nellie asked.

Gareth groaned. At least he'd managed to stay on his feet this time.

A SENSE of vertigo hit Catherine with so much power that she went weak in the knees, and they started to buckle.

"I don't think I can stand," she groaned, clinging to Gareth.

"I have you." He stiffened his arms around her, moaning himself.

His voice was so tight that it pulled Catherine from her own discomfort. She forced her eyes open and looked up at him. His pale face was dotted with perspiration.

"Nellie, take the portrait," Catherine cried. "And get him the potion. He's going to vomit."

"I am *not,*" Gareth said through gritted teeth.

Her own legs were still unsteady, but she forced herself to stand straighter so he didn't have to use his strength to support her. For a second, she thought they might both lose the battle and collapse to the floor. Then the painting was gone from against her back, and he pulled her closer.

"How could you face doing this again?" she mumbled. "It's awful."

"A sip of this will help, miss," a woman's voice said from Catherine's side, "and you'll be right as rain."

Catherine was afraid if she let go of Gareth that she might fall. The maid put the cup to Catherine's lips, and she took a sip. That wonderful feeling she remembered from the tonic Walter had given her in the car pushed back the dizziness. She took another sip and felt even better.

"Gareth?" she asked.

He'd dropped one hand from her back and was taking his cup from a man servant. Evidently, a gentleman of this time had to appear strong and couldn't accept somebody holding his teacup for them. It made her giggle.

Gareth looked at her with narrowed eyes and then drained the cup. After a shudder, he returned it.

"It's good to see you again, Geoffrey," Gareth said.

"As you say, my Lord," the man replied, a faint smile twitching at the corners of his mouth. "I assume I assisted you in the future."

"And did an excellent job." Gareth glanced down at Catherine. "Are you able to stand on your own?"

"I think so." Catherine lowered her voice. "Though I kind of like where I'm at."

Gareth grinned, and Aunt Nellie coughed.

"Yes, I do believe it would be a good thing for this young lady to stand on her own." She put an arm around Catherine's shoulders and gently pulled her away from Gareth. "I see you're also dressed for the ball. Very good. They have just finished dining. Dancing should begin again soon, if you both desire to join them."

"Is my sister still here?" Gareth asked. "She mentioned staying the night."

"Yes, that is correct. She did remark on your absence at dinner. I assured her you were fine and would join her later."

"How long before we feel normal enough to dance?" Catherine found herself a little excited to dance in this time to see if her experience at the Twickenham balls had prepared her enough.

"While the full effect comes after some sleep, you should be strong enough to participate should you so desire." Aunt Nellie tapped her chin in that familiar motion. She pointed to Catherine's portrait. "I did not expect you to bring back a guest, my Lord."

"Where are my manners?" Gareth already looked much better and took on the stilted manner he'd used when they first met. "May I introduce Doctor Catherine Ryan to you, Aunt Nellie?" He gave a dark laugh and added, "The Aunt Nellie from 1850."

"It's a pleasure, doctor." Nellie curtsied. "Are you here to stay?"

"No, just for a visit." Catherine gave Gareth a sidelong glance. "We had a traumatic experience today. Gareth got some public exposure that your future-self thought was a bad thing. Since he didn't want to do anymore sightseeing, she—*you* agreed that coming back would be good."

"And your memories are intact, my lord?" Aunt Nellie watched him with narrowed eyes.

"They are." He seemed to stand a little straighter, as though his response were a matter of honor.

"Well done, my Lord."

"As she's discovered this on her own, am I free to speak to her of those other things?" he asked.

"Yes, I believe so." Aunt Nellie turned her attention to Catherine. "And I suppose I should congratulate you on having unraveled our little secret, doctor. My future-self should have made it clear that your discretion in this matter is required."

"That goes without saying," Catherine said.

"It doesn't happen often, and I find it interesting that his Lordship did so on his own as well. You make an interesting pair."

"He was a man out of time." Biting back a smile, Catherine slid her hand into Gareth's.

Aunt Nellie frowned at them. "Yes, but you must understand we have much stricter rules here about conduct between unmarried men and women which you must abide by while you are here. One is that you must not refer to his Lordship by his given name. Another is you must not hold his hand." She pulled them apart, and stepped between them.

"In company, yes." Catherine sighed. This was going to be a little more complicated than she'd originally thought. "I've read some historical novels, but I may need some help to make sure I don't make things awkward for Gareth. Um, his Lordship."

"I will assign Lulu as your maid. She will assist you and watch to make sure you don't misstep." Aunt Nellie laughed softly. "She's had recent experience with a recalcitrant American visitor."

"Why do you assume I'm going to be recalcitrant?" Catherine asked, irritated. "That's a little presumptuous considering that we've just met."

"Perhaps. Americans do tend to be a bit . . . independent." Nellie's tone had taken on a teasing note, but there was an edge there that Catherine was already familiar with.

"Well, I'm kind of a hybrid," she said. "My grandparents came from England originally. I was born in the US and lived there until I was fifteen when we moved back."

"And yet you've maintained your American accent."

"On purpose." Catherine gave a little shrug. "I can talk like most Londoners if I choose to and sometimes do. I may have gone to medical school in England and practice there, but I'll never forget that I'm American by birth."

"Might I inquire why you returned with his Lordship, my dear?" Aunt Nellie asked. "Aside from this bad experience you both had."

Gareth watched Catherine, working too hard to keep his expression neutral. She knew in her heart that her answer was important to him. Well, it was important to her too.

"Because this month I made a very dear friend, who risked his life to save mine. Since he wanted to come home and invited me for a visit, I accepted." She didn't try to hide the pain in her expression. "I'm looking forward to having something else to think about than what happened today."

"I am curious about this, but it is clear to me that you both wish to forget. Perhaps in a few days." Aunt Nellie gave a soft nod. "*Do* you wish to attend the ball?"

Catherine glanced at Gareth.

"It is up to you, Miss Ryan," he said.

"I'd like to stay long enough for a dance or two, my Lord." Catherine held his gaze. "I'm not ready to leave you yet."

"As you say." His smile warmed her right to her toes.

15

"NOW, MISS," LULU SAID, AS she helped Catherine dress the next morning, "I heard you cry out last night. Aunt Nellie did say that you and his Lordship were part of something terrible. Tonight, I'll have a nice tea to help you sleep peacefully. I promise."

"That would be wonderful. I didn't rest very well last night." Catherine wondered if Gareth had been bothered with nightmares too. She hoped the man she'd been treating when the police arrived would be all right.

"Well, if you need to rest this afternoon, you have only to say so."

Catherine found she liked being pampered. It was like the spa weekend she and a couple of other women in her class had taken when they'd graduated from medical school.

"I overheard his Lordship mention a picnic once the weather is fine."

"Is it still raining?"

"Off and on, miss." Lulu straightened the back of the gown. "Once we have your hair done, you're to join him to break your fast."

"He *did* stay the night?"

"'Tis not uncommon for guests to do so as the balls end in the wee hours of the morning. The storm didn't help. Now, miss, if you'll sit, I will start on your hair." Lulu gestured for the dressing table chair. "Also, a word to the wise. Last night you thanked the servants a bit too much."

"Is that a bad thing?" Catherine sat, watching in fascination as the little maid began to swiftly turn her long hair into a fashionable 1850 updo.

"Now you sound like Miss Clarisse. She wasn't one to have people do for her. A go-getter, she was."

"Was she a time traveler too?"

"Oh, aye. She became fast friends with Lady Ellen and then his Lordship." Lulu paused, a crease appearing between her brows. "I think I should not have mentioned her."

"It's all right," Catherine said carefully, having been the recipient of unintended confidences in the past. "I think I may have met one of her friends, an American named Jem Taylor."

"You know Master Jem?" Lulu's entire countenance seemed to light up.

"We danced at last month's ball." Catherine's curiosity-itch had come alive, and her instincts told her the Americans had been important to Gareth and in a way that was important to Catherine too. "He said he was practicing his English accent."

"Oh, aye, and he did a fine job while he was here. He even went below stairs so he could learn the way we talk so he could masquerade as one of us while working on his Lordship's tenant village." Lulu let out a deep sigh. "Miss Clarisse made a difference there. We all did. There you are, miss, all ready for the day."

"What was Clarisse to his Lordship?" Catherine held the maid's gaze through the dressing table mirror.

The young woman's cheeks flushed. Catherine rose and turned around.

"Please, I need to know what I'm dealing with. Did this Clarisse mean something to him?"

"Aye, miss, but she chose Master Jem."

Gareth had been interested in this Clarisse then. Catherine thought Jem had been a charming young man, but why would anyone choose him over the earl?

"People of this time often make decisions quickly in matters of the heart," Lulu said. "Aunt Nellie mentioned this morning that you escorted his Lordship around your London."

"That's right."

"Then 'tis the magic, miss. Do not judge him harshly for having been temporarily distracted by Miss Clarisse. She awakened him from a living death left by the loss of his wife and son all those years ago."

Catherine's heart gave a sharp twist. So he'd been married before and lost them too. That explained the pain in his eyes.

"If you work with the magic, he can do the same for you." The little maid gave Catherine a shrewd glance.

A chill went down her back. How could the maid know Catherine had suffered a similar loss?

"Let me guide you to the breakfast room, miss." Lulu pointed to the bedroom door.

"I hope I don't go tumbling down the stairs in these," Catherine grumbled as they descended the broad staircase. She wasn't sure she liked the heavy petticoats. Thank heavens she wasn't wearing a crinoline like the one Scarlet O'Hara had worn in *Gone with the Wind*. It was still hard for Catherine not to imagine tumbling down the stairs like that heroine had done in the film.

"My dear," Aunt Nellie said from the bottom of the stairs, "might I have a word with you before you join his Lordship?"

"Certainly." Catherine gave a small curtsy, and Aunt Nellie nodded in approval and led the way to an office.

"Please be seated." Her hostess went around the desk and sat, so Catherine took the padded wooden chair in front of it. Aunt Nellie asked, "How did you sleep?"

"Not well, as I'm sure Lulu will tell you. She said she'll prepare a tea to help me rest better tonight."

"We should have anticipated that, and I do apologize. I had not realized the severity of what you and his Lordship survived. I spoke with him this morning and found that he also did not sleep well. We will be sure to provide you with the holiday you need to recover."

"Thank you. That's what I'm hoping for."

Aunt Nellie didn't say anything else for a while, long enough that it started to make Catherine uncomfortable. She had to force herself not to fidget and couldn't help feeling that she was being tested.

"You have pretty manners for someone from your time," Nellie finally said, "but I believe you should still have some instruction on deportment. It is not uncommon for our visitors from the future to require some lessons." She gave a soft laugh. "Some more than others."

"Like Clarisse?" Catherine wanted to bite back the words when Aunt Nellie's eyes flashed, her customary sense of humor gone.

"How would you know about her? Did one of the servants say something?"

"I met Jem Taylor at your ball in my time the night they traveled here and saw them when they returned. It's one of the reasons you painted my portrait."

Aunt Nellie let out a breath. "All of our time travelers have a way of leaving their mark on us, and Clarisse and Jem did that with the Hildebrand family."

"Should I know more?" Catherine asked.

"I believe that is something best left to his Lordship." Aunt Nellie clasped her hands and rested them on her desk. "As you will be breakfasting with him and will wish to spend the morning in his company, we should plan on your comportment lessons for this afternoon. I will be paying calls this morning, but I believe it best not to subject you to that quite yet."

"I will trust in your judgement." Catherine knew she'd taken the right approach when Nellie smiled.

"Very prettily said. Yes, I believe you will do well with a little added refining. You have a natural reserve that fits well with how a lady of quality should behave. Now, I believe his Lordship is anxious to see you."

With that dismissal, Catherine rose and left the office. Lulu waited outside.

"This way, miss."

Catherine entered the room alone and paused when she found a stranger inside. The handsome young man rose and bowed when he saw her.

"I believe you must be my aunt's guest from the future. Allow me to introduce myself. I'm William Milton."

"It's a pleasure to meet you." Catherine curtsied.

"We serve ourselves from the sideboard, so please help yourself." He indicated the row of covered dishes along the wall. "I hope you'll join me as you eat."

"Have you seen Gare— Lord Hildebrand yet?" Catherine would have to do better at that.

"Not yet." William tilted his head toward her. "Nice recovery."

"I don't want to do anything that would embarrass him or Aunt Nellie." Catherine gestured for him to sit. "I'd be happy to join you."

"It is an easier adjustment for some of our guests than for others." He took his seat again but didn't resume eating.

"I already miss comfortable clothes," Catherine said as she added food to her plate. "I imagine I'll get used to it by the time I leave in a few weeks."

"A few weeks?" William asked, a touch of humor to his voice.

"What do you mean?" She sat at his table, fighting the unease that came with his question.

"A few of our guests choose to stay in the time they visit." He picked up his fork.

"Do many people do that?" she asked.

"A fair number of those who find love do. Also, not all of our guests are pulled into the past. Sometimes they find themselves in the future. For example, one of the people I visited on my recent trip came here from four hundred years ago. She found she enjoyed our modern amenities and chose to stay."

"She didn't stay for love?"

"No, but she has found it since."

"But doesn't her being here risk changing the future?"

"Time is a fuzzball." William chuckled. "As my aunt is fond of saying, 'If it happened, it happened.'"

Catherine felt some relief in that. She wanted to meet people of this time and talk with them, but she'd been a little worried that she might break the future.

"I can understand someone wanting to stay in the future," she said. "It'd be hard to do the opposite though."

"Really?" He wiped his mouth. "What is it about this time that bothers you the most?"

"I'm a physician. It's the only thing I've ever wanted to do, and I love it. In this time, you don't have female doctors. I can't imagine living in a place where I couldn't practice medicine." She shifted the food around her plate, recalling Gareth's expression after the terrorist attack and then later when they'd returned to Nellie's house. He'd been adamant that he was ready to come back to his time. He wouldn't want to stay in the future.

Catherine forced herself to face the fact that when she left here to go back home, it might be the last time she would see him. Her heart gave that odd twist, and she rubbed her chest. No. She wouldn't think about it. All she wanted was this holiday. She'd enjoy Gareth's company while she had it and go back home to face the aftermath of the terrorist attack.

"You seem thoughtful," William said.

"I was just thinking about what I'll face when I go home."

"Ah, yes, my aunt mentioned you would have to deal with some unpleasant notoriety. She didn't go into detail. Is it something you can tell me?"

Catherine frowned. Except for talking to Nellie when they'd first arrived, she hadn't spoken of it to anyone, not even Gareth. Maybe it was time to find out how much she could handle. She swallowed and told William about the attack.

"Unfortunately, it's soured Gareth on my time. I'm not sure he'll ever want to visit there again." Catherine glanced at William and found his sympathetic gaze on her. She asked, "Could someone like him come to the future and stay?"

"It's possible, but unlikely," William said. "He's an earl and has responsibilities in this time, especially to his sister. Even when she marries, he has no heir yet. His Lordship is not a man to walk away from his responsibilities."

Catherine nodded. She'd thought that about Gareth. Hearing it confirmed made her sad, sadder than was safe for her heart.

"I BELIEVE I'll shave myself this morning," Gareth told Geoffrey.

"Becoming a modern man, my Lord?" the valet asked. "Be careful not to cut your throat."

"As Catherine . . . Miss Ryan would say—that would definitely ruin my day." While Gareth had enjoyed the ease of the modern shaving devices, he had missed the closer shave of a good straight-edge.

"Might I ask if you've done this before, my Lord?" Geoffrey hovered by Gareth's side, watching as he worked up a foam with the shaving brush.

"Not in this time, but I've found I enjoy the independence of doing certain things for myself." Gareth spread the foam on his face.

"My Lord, I would feel better if you were to allow me to first show you how to do it without injuring yourself."

"Afraid I'll cut my throat?"

"Exactly, my Lord."

Gareth hesitated, but the poor valet looked sincerely worried, so he handed the brush to the man.

"Thank you, my Lord," Geoffrey said with relief.

The valet did a good job and provided a detailed explanation of the process. When he was finished, Gareth ran a hand over his cheeks. He nodded his approval.

Before his journey to the future, he would have sent his groom back to Kellworth last night to collect his valet and several changes of clothing. The man wouldn't understand Gareth's new relaxed attitude about his dress. He wanted a little time to adjust to being back in his own time, so he'd opted to accept Aunt Nellie's offer to provide for his needs until the next day.

As Gareth tied his cravat, he thought back on his sister's surprise and pleasure at his overly enthusiastic greeting the night before. She'd also been pleased to meet Catherine.

Catherine. How long would it be before he could hold her in his arms again? Aunt Nellie had been overly watchful last evening. As soon as he'd finished his second dance with the good doctor, their hostess had been there, suggesting it was time for them both to retire.

He anticipated he would find the fae woman resistant if he invited Catherine to come for a visit to Kellworth. How long would she stay in this time? Long enough to determine if they suited?

Gareth thought perhaps Aunt Nellie would want to keep Catherine under observation until the doctor had proven her discretion. So be it.

When he entered the breakfast room, he found that Catherine

was not alone.

"Good morning, Miss Ryan." Gareth bowed.

Catherine had risen and made a lovely curtsy. "Good morning, your Lordship."

"Nicely done." He already missed the easy familiarity of her time and wished he could take her hand.

"You too, my Lord." She shot him a coy smile. "Why, it's almost as though you've been doing it your entire life."

"Well, I can see you two are great friends," William said with a chuckle.

"How are you Milton?" Gareth asked. "I hadn't heard you'd returned. Where did your travels take you this time?"

"Brighton."

"Did you visit the beach?" Gareth started serving himself from the sideboard.

"It was too short a trip for leisure."

"Do you like Brighton?" Catherine asked.

"When Ellen was younger, we would spend part of the summer there." Gareth sat beside her, edging his chair close to hers. "Until I discovered that she hates the beach."

"Oh no," she said with a laugh. "Do you not like the beach either?"

"Not particularly. I prefer to be active."

"There's plenty to do at the beach and not just lie in the sun," Catherine said. "It's probably just as well I didn't take you there in my time."

"I must leave you two." William rose. He took Catherine's hand and bowed over it. "I hope you enjoy your time with us. Good to see you again, Kellworth." He nodded to Gareth and strode from the room. A servant quietly removed his dishes.

"Have you considered what you might like to do today?" Gareth asked. "Our options are limited until the weather improves, but then we can go for ride. I would enjoy showing you the countryside and thought to take you on a picnic."

"I hope when you say ride that you mean in a carriage, my Lord, because I've never been on a horse."

"Do you speak the truth?"

"I'm not lying to you," she said, a charming furrow between her brows. "Our family wasn't wealthy, and my father used the time here to work on his book. We couldn't afford luxuries like riding lessons, much less the purchase and care of a horse."

"Perhaps a riding lesson is in order then," Gareth said. "At some point during your stay, I would also like to show you Kellworth."

"Is that your home?"

"Yes, it's our seat now as it's better situated to London, and the weather is milder here." He hesitated. "I was married, when I was fairly young. I confess that my father had his eye on the estate when he first suggested a meeting between myself and Cecily."

Catherine appreciated that he finally felt ready to share this with her. She was curious about this woman he'd cared so much for.

"Cecily is a lovely name," Catherine said carefully. "She brought the house with her into your marriage?"

"Yes, it was her dowry, property her mother brought into her own marriage."

"What happened to her?" Catherine asked, her voice gentle.

"She died in childbirth," he said, his voice soft. "When I first expressed interest in making it the family seat, it pleased her father because his grandchildren would eventually own it as well as my title."

"Oh, that's so sad." Her eyes glistened with compassion. "Was she an only child or did he have other children?"

"He has two sons and several grandchildren now." Gareth arched a brow, unable to keep the bitterness from his tone. "No title though, for which he was sorely disappointed."

"He was more concerned about the title than his daughter?"

Her look of disgust filled him with satisfaction. Catherine's indignation reminded him again of Reese. He thought if they had met in their own time that they might have been friends. The image rather appealed to him.

"You must understand that not all parents are doting."

"Well, that's true enough, even in my time. I had a—"

"Ah, Gareth, I'm afraid I must leave early," Ellen said, sweeping into the dining room.

He stood and accepted his sister's kiss on the cheek. When Catherine struggled to rise, he pulled out her chair.

"Lady Ellen." She curtsied.

"It is lovely to see you again, Miss Catherine." Ellen took her hands. "I had hoped to get to know you better, but in spite of a house full of servants to boss around, our Grandmama has insisted that I assist her in the move to the Kellworth dower house."

Catherine laughed. "I remember my own grandmother doing that to my mother."

"I hope that my brother will not also receive a summons. I must be off." Ellen turned and left the room, giving her maid instructions as they went.

"Should you go with her?" Catherine asked, taking her seat again.

"I would be in their way." Gareth returned to the sideboard. "Have you considered my offer to teach you to ride?"

"If I could wear jeans, I might think about it."

"I confess that I would not mind seeing you in jeans again." He arched a brow, his expression flirty, and she laughed. Gareth added, "I believe Aunt Nellie's dressmaker has a split-skirt habit that she made at the request of other modern travelers. If you wish to ride astride, I'm sure they could accommodate you."

"I think I'd rather learn to drive a horse than ride one."

"Would you? How fortunate that I am just the man to assist you in that." He took his seat beside her, frowning at the servant standing to the side. Gareth leaned closer to Catherine, covering her hand with his, and whispered, "I miss being able to speak privately with you."

"Well, I'm free this morning. This afternoon I have Aunt Nellie's comportment lesson." Catherine rolled her eyes, though her cheeks had flushed, he hoped from his touch.

IT RAINED for three blissful days. Catherine and Gareth investigated the manor and spent time studying the portraits.

"I know several of these people," he said, staring at the wall. "I had wondered if there were other time travelers."

"Now you know." Catherine said, standing close to him, her fingers wrapped around his in the cover of her skirt, so the maid following at a discrete distance couldn't see. At least there was some good in having to wear all that fabric. "I wonder what their stories are."

"Do I dare broach the subject with them?" Gareth looked down at her, his expression amused. Then his gaze drifted to her mouth.

Catherine's senses went on high alert, electricity sparking between them. She leaned closer, her chin lifted.

Lulu coughed.

"Perhaps not." Gareth faced the wall again.

Catherine didn't know if he meant it in answer to his question or to the almost-kiss. She sighed, and they continued the tour of the house.

They ended up in the library which began their pattern for rainy days. Sometimes they'd sit at a table playing chess or the card game Snap. Catherine had been surprised to find it was almost the same as one she'd played as a girl. She was very good at it. They both had fast reflexes, so the competition was fierce. The only advantage Gareth had was his longer arms which gave him a better reach.

Other times they would curl up on a loveseat before the fire, taking turns reading to each other, always with Lulu or some other servant quietly mending in a corner of the room. Their watchdog would cough or say something if they snuggled too closely or looked about to kiss.

Catherine visited Aunt Nellie in the afternoons, learning how to behave like a lady of quality. Some things came more easily to Catherine, and she thought the pleasant manners she'd had to use as a doctor helped. The evenings were spent with whomever happened to be staying at the manor at the time. It seemed like the fae woman had an ongoing house party with guests coming and going.

The lazy days were just what Catherine needed. The tea worked wonderfully, and her sleep was dreamless. She slept in, took long baths, and was wonderfully pampered. In spite of the continued gloomy skies, she woke every morning knowing that she'd see Gareth soon, and her day brightened.

The first day it didn't rain, he mentioned riding again or going on a picnic.

"Won't the ground be soggy?" Catherine asked, hating for their idyll to come to an end.

"True," Gareth said. "If the sun dries it out enough today, perhaps tomorrow."

"You're anxious to get outside." She knew he was getting restless and remembered that he'd mentioned liking to be active. Since guys of this time didn't have a gym to work out in, that must be how they got their exercise.

"I confess I am, though I have enjoyed this quiet time with you." Gareth brushed aside a strand of hair from her cheek and let his fingers rest there until the maid coughed.

"This is killing me," Catherine said, keeping her voice soft.

"I as well." Gareth dropped his hand. "I will hope for a warm day today then and look forward to getting outside. For now, a game of Snap?" He offered Catherine his arm, and she took it.

"I would love to."

16

"I BETTER NOT EMBARRASS MYSELF," Catherine said to Lulu as the maid handed over her riding gloves. "Or kill the earl."

"Or yourself, miss. Have no fear. His Lordship is a noted whip, so you have nothing to fear."

Catherine let out a nervous breath. "If you say so." The servant opened the front door, and she stepped into the bright sunshine, wishing for a decent pair of sunglasses instead of the hat she had to wear instead.

Gareth stood by the carriage, looking handsome. His smile warmed her all the way through. He was even more attractive in his own time because he fit here. His increased confidence added to his attractiveness. Which was saying something.

"Miss Catherine." He bowed and glanced at the Twickenham servants going about their business. "Do you wish for your first lesson here?"

"No, my Lord." She appreciated his discretion. "I believe it might be better if you show me how it's done. That would be much better than turning the reins over to an untrained novice who's likely to be a menace to everyone around her."

A twinkle sparkled in Gareth's eyes as he extended his hand to help her up.

She glanced from it to her skirts and then to the curricle. When she fingered the heavy petticoat underneath, considering how she could fit in the seat space with all that fabric, he chuckled.

"Don't laugh at me," she hissed, trying not to laugh herself. "This is a ridiculous fashion."

"It will fit. If necessary, your skirt can overflow into my lap."

"All right." Catherine accepted his hand, wishing she wouldn't have to let it go. She waited to sit until he was in place, and the skirt fell into position more easily than she'd expected. "Believe it or not, skirts are going to get so wide women will need metal hoops to keep them up for them. They'll get so big that some women will have a hard time getting through doorways."

"Truly?" Gareth shot her a considering sidelong glance. "I imagine that kind of knowledge could prove useful."

"You're already rich, so forget it."

His eyes crinkled at the corners, and he indicated a blanket the groom was holding out to her. "I doubt the roads will be dusty yet, but you may use it to cover your dress if you wish."

"I'm not afraid of a little dirt," she said.

"No, but it could ruin the dress."

"Good point." Catherine spread the blanket over her skirt. She hoped it didn't make her hot enough to start sweating since they didn't have deodorant here.

"You hold the reins in the left hand," Gareth said demonstrating, "separated by the first and second fingers and held by the third and fourth ones. You'll use it to control the speed of the horse, and the reins can be used to steer when your right hand is busy."

"But what if I do something wrong, and the horse takes off?"

"My dear, if you could learn to be a doctor, you can drive a carriage. Now, the whip should always be in your right hand. If it's needed for safety, you'll have it immediately."

Catherine listened, knowing there was no way she'd pick this up quickly. She reminded herself that she hadn't learned to drive a car in one lesson either. Of course, cars didn't have minds of their own.

Her head had started to hurt a little by the time Gareth pulled off the road and into a meadow full of what looked like a wide variety of wildflowers.

"It's beautiful," Catherine breathed. "Is this property yours?"

"No, it's part of the Twickenham estate, though my sister has been inspired to create something like it at Kellworth."

After the groom leaped to the ground and hurried to hold the horse's head, Gareth jumped off. He extended both of his hands, the corners of his mouth quirking up. His expression told her he was up to something, and a little thrill ran through her. She set aside the light blanket and stood.

Gareth took her by the waist and, as he lifted her from the carriage, she was struck again by how strong he was. He took his time easing her down and paused when their faces were level. His lips barely brushed hers as they passed. That briefest of touches sent a shiver of pleasure through her. By the time Catherine's feet touched the ground, they were standing close enough that she could feel the pounding of his heart. It matched the mad rhythm of her own.

She inhaled, loving the way he smelled. There was something so masculine about the combination of leather, the scent he wore, and *him* that set her heart racing. She lifted her hand and cupped his cheek, running a thumb over his lips, her entire body pulsing.

"Catherine." The single word came out gruffly. Gareth coughed and released her, stepping back. He whispered, "We are not alone."

"Right. I'll get the blanket." Her body was hot now with embarrassment. What must that boy be thinking of them? Besides, she wasn't staying here, and she was walking a fine line. It wouldn't do to get too attached and then be hurt.

Catherine made her way to an area with more grass than flowers and spread it out. She scanned the horizon, heady with the warmth of the August sunshine and the sweet perfume of the blooms. The lack of modern noises—mobiles, automobiles, or air planes—drove home *when* she was.

It held an allure she hadn't anticipated and reminded her of picnics with her grandmother when they'd first moved to England. Catherine had raved about how beautiful the biblical Garden of Eden must have been. Grandma had grinned.

"And just like the Garden of Eden, this one also has a serpent." She'd pointed to a snake slithering away from them.

Catherine glanced to where Gareth held the basket and was saying something to the groom. How funny that a memory of her dead grandmother should provide such a perfect analogy. The earl did provide a strong temptation.

"You may take your meal over there." Gareth pointed to the other side of the curricle, and the groom took his food with him.

"Well, at least with all these petticoats I'll have my own padding." Catherine crossed her ankles and sat. The skirt still kind of bubbled up like a balloon. It reminded her a little of being a kid in a swimming pool and playing with T-shirt air pockets. She laughed and pushed on the fabric, flattening it.

"What do you find humorous?" Gareth asked, setting down the basket beside the blanket.

She explained. "It's odd figuring out how to get around in the clothing of this time."

"I can say the same thing for your future styles." Gareth took off his riding jacket and carefully folded it before putting it on the ground. He caught her watching him and shrugged. "My man would have a fit of apoplexy."

"A stroke? Wow. He really takes his job seriously."

"He has status because he serves an earl and takes pride in doing it well."

"That'll only last a few more decades." Catherine opened the basket to see what was included. "A nice loaf of bread. Do you have sandwiches in this time?"

"Of course we do." Gareth sounded a little insulted as he went down on his knees, close to the basket. He leaned forward at the same time she did, and his hair brushed her face.

Catherine pulled back so they didn't bump heads but also because he smelled intoxicating. There was so much about this man that enticed her—his wit, his kindness, his sheer physical presence. She thought of her grandmother's favorite Benjamin Franklin quote. *If passion drives . . .*

". . . Let reason hold the reins," Catherine finished the saying aloud, raising her hands as though she held a wall between herself and Gareth. At his startled expression, she burst out laughing. She explained, "Don't worry. It was a compliment. Now tell me about this food. I'm getting hungry."

A furrow had appeared between Gareth's brow as he pulled out a cloth and spread it between them. When he'd emptied the basket, they had the makings for sandwiches, some fruit tarts for dessert, and a bottle with what turned out to be lemonade.

He remained quiet as they prepared and then ate their food. She wondered if she'd hurt his feelings and didn't know how to fix it without telling him just how attracted to him she was. Gareth Hildebrand was coming to mean a lot to her, and he could be persuasive. Too persuasive for a woman who was falling hard for him. It didn't feel safe to put that little bit of information in his hands, not if she was determined to return to her own time.

GARETH HAD SENSED Catherine pull back emotionally. He hadn't found her reticent about his attentions before coming to his time.

Could that have come from the trauma they were both recovering from? She had mentioned something in passing, a string of letters he couldn't recall that had referred to it.

He wished only for them to become better acquainted. Perhaps then, her doubts could be put to rest.

"You have said you're not wealthy," Gareth finally said. "Yet you were able to receive training to become a physician. Did you apprentice yourself?"

"We don't do the apprentice thing. We have medical schools, and it takes years of study. We understand a lot more in my time than in yours. There's tons to learn, and the body's complicated. Diseases for one patient don't necessarily manifest the same in another." She continued to speak as she started placing the items back in the basket. "We also have specialties. For example, people with heart problems will see a cardiologist. Someone with cancer, an oncologist. I specialized in emergency care, for people who need attention immediately."

"It's fortunate then that you were there during the attack."

"And that I had a companion who knew how to use a cane like you did." She met his gaze, hers troubled. "It's also fortunate that first responders were so fast. I won't know until I go home how many people were killed and injured. I'm kind of glad that Aunt Nellie didn't tell us that."

Catherine shuddered, and he shifted so he sat beside her. Resisting the urge to put his arm around her shoulders because of propriety, he only took her hand.

"If one must attend this school of medicine for many years, how does one pay? Did you have a sponsor?"

"No." She smiled. "There are grants, scholarships if you can qualify, and loans. When my grandmother died, it turned out she'd had an education savings account for me. It helped, but I spent a lot of time in school, so it's taken a while to pay off my student loans. That's one of the reasons I've lived so simply."

Pain had returned to her voice. Did it embarrass her to have been poor? Was the difference between their stations the cause for her to hold back from him? No. He had not seen that concern in her time. Then what? Perhaps it was this grandmother she had mentioned.

"Are you close to your family?" he asked.

"I was." Her voice cracked on the last word, and her eyes filled.

"Catherine," Gareth said, "I asked you before if you were alone. Is your family no longer with you?"

"They're all gone," she whispered. "I'm both a widow and an orphan. If I'd died in that attack, it would have been the end of my family."

"Ah, you too then. Will you tell me how you lost your husband and family?"

Catherine closed her eyes, her throat working. He was tempted to tell her she need not speak of it, but he sensed that it was important that she do so.

"And our daughter. Diana. She was two and so beautiful. My father had finally sold his book. To celebrate, he took the family on holiday to Cornwall. Dad had plans to check out the area because he wanted to write about the history there. It'd been raining a lot. When it cleared for a little while, they decided to get out of the hotel rooms, especially the baby. I was supposed to go with them, but I didn't feel well and stayed behind." Her voice broke, and she had to choke out the next words. "In a freak of nature, a flash flood hit the town. A wall of water swept them away. It took a week before they were able to recover all their bodies."

Throwing off propriety, Gareth pulled her into his arms then and held her. He remembered the anguish of the day Cecily and their son had died. How much worse would his grief have been had he known his son as Catherine had known her daughter? He held her until she calmed.

"This is why I don't talk about it. I fall apart." Wiping her eyes,

Catherine straightened but stayed close to him, as though she still needed his support. "I should have been with them."

"Had you been," Gareth said, handing her one of his handkerchiefs, "you would have died too."

Catherine didn't say more, merely resting against him. Gareth gathered his own courage.

"As I told you before, I was also married." He ignored the way she shifted, not wanting to look at her as he spoke. "We'd been wed nearly a year when she gave birth to our son. He came early. There was too much bleeding."

"She hemorrhaged," Catherine shifted and took his hand.

Gareth nodded. "They couldn't stop it. Then, our son had trouble breathing and didn't survive her by even three hours."

"Probably Lung Hypoplasia. I'm so sorry," she whispered. "How long ago?"

"Ten years."

"And you've never remarried?"

Gareth shook his head. He had no words to explain the madness that had gripped him, of how rash he'd become, how stupid. His recent glimpse at his own mortality had wakened him to the risk in which he'd also put Ellen. It made him sick.

"How long since your loss?" he asked.

"Not quite two years. I've gotten through by focusing on my work and nothing else. I've picked up extra shifts, so I didn't have to go home to my empty flat. It's only lately that I've allowed myself to do something else. That's when I started attending Aunt Nellie's balls."

"And took a holiday to the past."

"Yes." Catherine gave him a wan smile. "This time I've spent with you . . . it's the first time I've let myself get close to anyone."

"I've spent ten years playing the fool. I have spent my time around frivolous people yet allowing none of them close to me." He touched his heart, and she met his gaze. There was the strong attraction, perhaps more powerful even than before, but there was a sense of understanding. “Catherine, you have changed something deep within me. I like to think that I may have done the same for you.”

“You have.” She looked down and whispered, “It scares me to death.”

Once again, Gareth understood. He reached over and gently lifted her chin. She met his gaze and recognized the battle going on in her eyes. It would be a simple thing for her to return to her time where he might never see her again.

“I understand.” He wanted to take her in his arms but sensed it would be wise to break the moment. “I believe the groom has fallen asleep.” Gareth rose to his feet and extended his hands to her. “We should return to the manor.”

“Good idea.”

17

THE PLEASANT DAYS OF PAMPERED leisure began to blend into each other. Catherine came to understand why people from her time would pay to spend a week immersed in the past at Aunt Nellie's. The gracious manners and outwardly polite society provided a pleasant balm on Catherine's raw nerves.

Twickenham always seemed to have guests coming and going, including one young man who'd arrived a little after Catherine and Gareth, though he'd traveled from 1973. William Milton had taken him in hand for a trip to Scotland to check on some time travelers there.

Gareth was frequently in attendance, but there were days she didn't see him. He did have an estate to run, after all. Ellen had sent him a request to come to Bath for a few days to assist with his grandmother's move. He'd invited Catherine to come, but Nellie had nixed it, saying she wasn't ready for wider society yet.

The deportment lessons each day weren't too bad. Aunt Nellie would have Catherine apply one day's lessons the next day while accepting callers. She couldn't help thinking that the lessons were more involved than they needed to be, almost as though her hostess was training Catherine for a role she'd need to play.

Fortunately, the week Gareth was gone, another party of six people had arrived from London for a stay. They were a pleasant group and made sure to invite her to join them in whatever activities they were involved in for the day. She frequently went with them, but it wasn't the same without Gareth, and it drove home how much she missed him.

"Miss Ryan, would you care to join us for some Whist?" Sir Jack Hughes Von Maughanhoe asked the first night Gareth had been able to join her again. Jack usually brought his cousin Amelia with him and had shown himself to be one of the flirts of the group. He reminded her of a harmless guy she'd known in school.

"Perhaps Miss Ryan would prefer a stroll outside," Gareth suggested. "It's a pleasant evening now the rain has stopped."

Catherine would have enjoyed a walk with him. It would be safer to stay with the others.

"The ground will still be too wet. I haven't played Whist before. Would you teach me?" She glanced at Jack. "If you don't mind playing against a novice."

"Of course not, Miss Ryan." He grinned. "It would be my pleasure to defeat you and his Lordship."

"If you wish." Gareth pulled out her chair and helped her sit before taking his own across from her. As he began with a basic overview of the game, he slid his foot next to hers. Was he playing footsy?

"This sounds a lot like Spades." When Jack shot her a curious look, Catherine added, "That's a game my grandmother liked to play."

She and Gareth partnered well, especially once she could remember the differences between the two games.

"I cannot but feel as though I have been given a Canterbury tale, Miss Ryan," Jack finally said after losing his third game.

"I'm sorry. I didn't mean to mislead you. I've really never played Whist before, but I've played Spades a lot."

Gareth smiled at her, looking pleased with himself. Jack leaned closer to him, his voice soft but still loud enough for her to hear.

"Will congratulations be in store soon, my Lord?"

Gareth didn't say anything but his gaze met hers, and the too-familiar warmth flooded through Catherine. If she'd had her fan with her, she'd have used it.

Jack coughed and straightened. "Yes, I believe so. Oh, good. Aunt Nellie has refreshments for us." He rose and went with his partner to the tray of desserts.

Catherine had never felt so conflicted in her life. It'd taken her over a year to fall in love with her husband. She'd only known Gareth for a couple of months. How was it possible that she could already feel so strongly about him? She needed to go home before she set herself up for terrible heartbreak. But going back to her time meant saying goodbye to him forever.

She was in serious trouble.

18

"MISS RYAN, ARE YOU ATTENDING me?" Aunt Nellie asked, looking like she'd been in the middle of speaking when she realized her student had zoned out.

"I'm sorry." Catherine arched her neck. "I'm a little distracted this afternoon." It was the night of the Full Moon Ball. Gareth had been urging her to stay another month because his sister had finally returned, and he wanted Catherine to come to Kellworth for a visit.

"You have done well with your deportment lessons. Perhaps today we should chat instead." Nellie put down the teapot. "If you are still having nightmares of that terrible experience—"

"No, it's not that. The tonic Lulu gave me the first few nights here has worked wonders. I was worried at first that they'd come back when I stopped taking it, but they haven't."

"Then what is troubling you, my dear?"

"I think it's time I went home."

"But I thought you'd received an invitation to stay at Kellworth."

Catherine closed her eyes at the sudden pain in her chest.

When she felt Aunt Nellie's hand cover hers, she opened them again.

"I do not often send people through time who have not accidentally traveled. When his Lordship came to me the day after I returned our American guests, the magic told me that he needed to visit your time. I also am not known to paint portraits for people who've not traveled accidentally, yet my future-self painted yours. It is no accident that the two of you have met."

"I can't stay here." Catherine's last word came out as a croak, and she had to rub at her throat before she could speak again. "I've wanted to be a doctor for half my life and invested a third of it in training to become one. There's no place for a female physician in this time."

"One of my most recent guests thought the same thing, yet her association with his Lordship and Lady Ellen has saved lives and changed the course for many others. Perhaps you should ask the earl to take you to visit his tenant village."

Be with Gareth alone? Catherine shook her head. He made her want things she knew she couldn't have.

"I don't believe you can make a good decision until you have more information. Truly, my dear, I have learned it is wise to work with the magic."

Catherine still didn't know what she thought about this idea of magic as a driving force in people's lives—outside of a faerie tale.

"All right, but I'd prefer not to go with him alone."

"Of course not." Aunt Nellie gave her an understanding smile. "I can imagine that the powerful connection between the two of you muddies your thoughts. You should talk with my other guests about making a party of it. His Lordship's cottiers now have the beginnings of a thriving business they might also enjoy seeing."

"Now have?"

"Yes, because of some of our more recent time travelers."

"The five Americans?"

"Two of them were involved in this project, though one in particular. Miss Clarisse Hamilton."

"*She* was involved in this?"

Aunt Nellie's smile transformed into an impish grin. Catherine's curiosity-itch came fully awake. It was obvious the woman knew something that she found . . . humorous? Catherine wanted to ask about it, but she had a strong feeling that she'd not get a satisfying answer.

"All right. I think I'd like to see this village."

Catherine left Nellie's office with a firm purpose in mind. The fae woman had been right that Catherine needed to make an informed decision. Every time she looked at Gareth, she knew what he had in mind; she could see it in his eyes. If they were ever alone again, with no threat that someone would interrupt them, she had no doubt that he would ask her to stay here permanently.

The worst was that a part of her would have liked to stay. It had been a struggle, but logic was winning the battle with her feelings. Catherine had dedicated too much of her life to being a doctor. It was part of her and not something she could simply walk away from for a man she'd known for a couple of months.

Catherine needed to tell him she was going home, but every time she thought about it, the words got all twisted with her heart. She wanted to be with Gareth, so much that the thought of leaving him caused her physical pain. But so did the thought of giving up being a doctor.

As she was coming down the hallway from Nellie's office, Sir Jack came skipping down the stairs. When he reached the bottom, he saw her and grinned. He took her hand and bowed, then gave a furtive scan of the room before kissing it.

"I have no desire to bring the wrath of the earl upon my shoulders," Jack said with a wink.

"You, sir, are a dreadful tease."

"You wound me." He put a dramatic hand over his chest.

"Someday, a lady is going to capture your heart, and you will be truly done in," Catherine said. "Now, to be serious. I'm tired of being in the house. Aunt Nellie suggested we go on an excursion."

"Excellent. What do you have in mind?"

"She mentioned that a tenant village has a new business venture that I might find interesting. It belongs to Lord Hildebrand, so we'll need his permission."

"Did I hear my name?" Gareth stepped out of the library, making her wonder if he'd been eavesdropping. He shot Jack a glare, and the young man stepped back in mock alarm.

"You two behave." Catherine repeated her explanation to Gareth. "Aunt Nellie said that another of her guests, a Clarisse Hamilton—" She paused for a second, watching Gareth for a response but couldn't tell if the twitch in his jaw was her imagination. "—was involved in it."

"My cottiers are doing something quite innovative, something that Miss Hamilton did indeed suggest." Gareth tapped his chin as though in thought, but Catherine was getting to know him well enough to recognize the playful quality to it. "I believe she called it a 'progressive business model,' something about how the quality of people's lives made a difference in the quality of the work they did. Progressive ideas, I know. She said workers performed their labors better when they were happy and well cared for, that it's important to see that they have good living conditions, training, and access to *health care*."

He shot Catherine a meaningful look, and she understood why Nellie had suggested this particular village. Yes, this might be a very good place for her to visit.

"I find myself intrigued," Jack said, serious for once, "as much for the idea itself as that you champion it, my Lord. I shall be interested to know if it is successful."

"If we brought food, is there a place where we could set up for tea?" Catherine asked.

"I believe so," Gareth said. "I will send my man to give them word to expect us. Their efforts are still in the infancy stage, so please be kind in your comments. Considering the state of the village a scant three months ago, they've made great progress."

"I will see who else in my party would like to join us," Jack said. "I hope the good weather holds."

"Regardless of what the others do, I would like to go. I'll see what I can do to help cook pull the food together," Catherine said, her mind already at work. "Sir Jack, if you would be so kind to send word to the kitchen once you know the number in our party, I'd appreciate it."

"It would be my pleasure." He bowed, turned, and strode away.

"It will be nice to be outside with you again, dear Catherine." Gareth took her hand and brought it to his lips.

Heaven help me. It took everything she had not to close the short distance between them and kiss him. What was she, some hormone-ridden teenager swooning over a cute boy in school? No, she was falling in love with an amazing man who had the ability to turn her brain into mush with a tender endearment.

She pinched her lips and gently pulled back her hand. The corners of his mouth twitched. He knew exactly the effect he had on her. It was so unfair.

"I'll go talk to cook." Catherine turned and went stiffly toward the kitchen, almost sure she heard him chuckle.

It took just over an hour to pull everything together. Aunt Nellie must have immediately sent orders for her carriage to be readied, which sat four people comfortably. The three men chose to ride their horses, leaving the three ladies to ride inside. A wagon followed with the food, dishes, and the staff to serve tea.

"So, you are his Lordship's latest flirt," one of the women said, the older of the two. "Be careful with your heart."

"Yes, do take care," the second woman said a little wistfully. "He has made it clear he never intends to marry again."

Catherine shrugged a shoulder. It didn't really matter because she wasn't staying anyway. But it did make her wonder what his intentions were.

The two women didn't say anything else about it, mostly talking among themselves. They were pleasant and tried to involve Catherine in their conversation. She did as much as she dared, not knowing enough about specific history. That would be something she'd have to study up on if she were to stay there.

The thought brought Catherine up short. It was the first time since she'd arrived that she'd really considered the possibility of staying. Were her emotions starting to gain traction over her logic?

She couldn't stay here, could she? She didn't fit, and she'd have to sacrifice so much to be with him. And yet, here she was traveling to his tenant village to see the effect that a modern woman could have on the lives of real people in this time. Was there a way to test it out first? Maybe she could visit him in this time and then return to the future and her job. Or was that just a way to put off the inevitable?

Catherine was glad when they finally approached a village, anything that would take her mind off the earl. He was at the door quickly, offering her his hand. She took his arm in that familiar way, loving the way he covered her hand with his. She'd paid attention to other couples who walked like this. His was definitely a more intimate gesture that even flirty Jack wouldn't use.

The residents had gathered as they approached. When they recognized Gareth, they curtsied or bowed. Catherine was impressed that he seemed to know them all by name and asked after their individual needs.

"I have a confession to make," he said softly as the others walked ahead. "Had you visited three months ago, you would have found a vile place filled with demoralized, sickly people."

"Why?"

"Because I had been negligent in my duties, insufferable in my self-importance." He didn't look at her, and she could tell the words were hard for him to speak. "Reese taught me to see things differently."

Reese? Clarisse? But hadn't Lulu said she was marrying Jem? Catherine pushed back a twinge of jealousy. It was stupid because she wasn't staying here anyway. She focused on what he was *really* saying.

"I'm proud of you for being teachable. It can be a hard thing."

"Indeed."

Catherine scanned the street, trying to imagine what it must have been like. Had it stunk? The place smelled like new construction now. In the distance, people were busy building a large structure.

"What's that?"

"Reese called it a community center, a place where the people could gather," Gareth said.

"Nice. Her idea, I assume?"

"Yes. It is an unusual concept but needed. For example, one cottier is a blind dressmaker who can no longer care for herself. She is conducting lessons on dressmaking but must do so in her small, dark cottage."

"And it'd be easier for them to hold lessons in a larger building."

"Exactly. We hope to have it completed before the first snow. I have contributed the lumber, and they are providing the labor for their share."

"Sweat equity," Catherine said, impressed. In her mind's eye she could imagine what the place must have looked like. The residents still showed signs of recovery, like people who'd been sick and were on the mend but weren't quite healthy yet. Gareth was doing good work here.

"What is sweat equity?" Jack asked, stepping beside Gareth.

"Equity is value you get from an investment. Sweat equity is like that." Catherine pointed to the community center. "The people add value to something by the sweat of their labors."

"Innovative indeed, my Lord." Jack nodded. "Is this what you have been talking to other landowners about?"

"It is."

"You've given me a lot to consider for my own property. For now, I'm hungry." Jack rubbed his hands together and headed to where the servants were setting up for tea.

Her mind busy, Catherine watched the workers. They'd been hopeless, helpless three months ago. Now they were full of optimism and drive. The change was as profound as night and day, cliché though the thought was.

"Catherine, I would speak to you before we join the others." Gareth's words were soft, hesitant.

Her stomach knotted at the same time that her heart started doing gymnastics. How could she want and not want something so powerfully at the same time? Her gaze shifted to the construction again. It'd come about because a modern woman had helped a man from this time to see things differently.

The more Catherine learned about this man, the more she respected him. He needed a woman at his side who could help him do more of this. She was a doctor who fully intended to keep practicing. People of his station would never accept her and, through her, him.

As she accepted that reality, a sharp pain slashed through her chest. It wasn't just about her. She could tease herself with thoughts of staying with him, but she didn't fit in here. If she stayed, she'd drag him down, kill the wonderful work he was doing.

"Kellworth, I need you," Sir Jack called, waving at the earl to come to the construction area.

"Gareth, no. Please don't," Catherine said, freeing her hand and stepping back. "This proves to me that I can't stay. You're doing great things here, and you need someone beside you who can help you to influence others to do more." She wiped at the moisture on her cheeks.

Instead of stopping him, her words seemed to fuel his determination. His eyes blazed.

"I *love* you, Catherine. I wish to marry you. Together we can make this work."

"Miss?" Lulu asked, coming up to them. "Are you not well?"

"I feel ill and need to go home."

"Catherine, please don't let this be the end." Gareth tried to take her hand again, but she stumbled away from him.

"I can't."

The depth of pain that flashed across his face was like another stab of a knife. How could it happen twice that her heart could be ripped from her while she was still breathing?

"Kellworth, are you coming?" Sir Jack strode toward them.

Lulu put her hand on Catherine's back, and she let the maid guide her to the carriage.

19

"I KNOW YOU NEED TO return to collect the others," Catherine said to Lulu as they drove up to Twickenham Manor. "I'm sorry that I've put you to so much trouble."

"'Tis not a problem, miss. We'll get you settled in your room, and I'll bring you some tea."

"You don't have a potion that'll fix what's wrong with me." Catherine opened the carriage door and climbed out on her own, hitting the ankle of her boot on the step, gasping with pain. "Where are the clothes I wore here?"

"Miss, you cannot do this to his Lordship." The little fae's voice had never been so stern.

Why couldn't they see what was so obvious to Catherine? She shook her head and limped to the house with Lulu calling orders to some of the other servants as she hurried after Catherine.

When she entered the house, Aunt Nellie was walking out of her office and stopped short. "What has happened?"

"I need you to send me home. *Now,* before they get back."

Her hostess hesitated for a moment as though she were listening to something, and then she heaved out a deep, sad sigh.

"Lulu, retrieve the clothing she wore upon her arrival. I'll see

Miss Ryan to her room." Aunt Nellie took her arm and helped her up the stairs. When they got to Catherine's room, she said, "Let me see what you've done to your leg."

"It's just my ankle, and it's fine. I can't be here when he gets back."

"I believe he's in love with you." Nellie undid the buttons down the dress's back. "Will you leave him without a word?"

"I don't have time. I have to leave."

"You, a healer, cannot make time to offer balm to a heart you're breaking?"

"Don't say that." Catherine clutched her hands to the pain in her chest. "I'll be the ruin of him if I stay."

Aunt Nellie said nothing but finished with the buttons. Lulu entered the room carrying Catherine's clothes. At least they weren't bloodstained. She stared at them for a second. It seemed surreal to be going back to the time right after the terrorist attack.

"Do you have some paper and a pen?" Catherine asked once she was dressed in the ball gown. She'd make sure to never wear one again. It'd be scrubs forever.

"Yes." Aunt Nellie indicated the small desk that Catherine had never bothered to use.

"Are you kidding me?" she asked when she saw the quill and a bottle of ink.

"Try this one, miss." Lulu pulled out what looked like an early version of a fountain pen.

"Can I have some privacy? I'll be quick and then join you in the portrait room," Catherine said as she sat at the desk.

"If you insist," Aunt Nellie said, and the two women left the room.

It didn't take long to write the words that would kill all hope for a future with Gareth. Rubbing at the ache in her chest, she read through the letter. A fat tear landed on the paper and made the ink run a little, but she didn't have time to rewrite it. She dabbed at the spot with her handkerchief, but it only smudged it more. After she'd folded it, she put it into an envelope. She had no idea how to seal it, so she wrote his name on the front.

Outside came the sound of wheels and people's laughing voices. She ran to the window. Gareth sat his horse so beautifully but he wore a frown. He glanced up toward the house. She stepped back, hoping he hadn't seen her.

Catherine held the envelope in place under her arm, picked up her skirts, and ran for the portrait room.

"Give this to Gareth for me," she said breathlessly, thrusting the envelope to Nellie and hurrying to stand in front of her picture.

"It sounds as though they've returned. Do you not wish—"

"No!" Catherine cried, her heart wrenching. "Please don't make me say goodbye to him again."

Aunt Nellie set down the envelope and took a handful of the dust she used for her magic. Catherine closed her eyes, barely aware of the increasing light. Then the sickening dizziness hit her, and she felt like she was falling back into the picture.

With a churning stomach, Catherine opened her eyes and found the familiar, modern Twickenham portrait room around her. She collapsed to the floor and started to cry.

GARETH SEARCHED the foyer for Catherine as he handed his hat to a servant upon their return to the manor. Perhaps she was still in her chambers. He was sure he'd seen her at the window and had hoped she would come downstairs to greet them.

"Might I have a word with you, your Lordship?" Aunt Nellie hurried down the stairs, slid her arm through his, and walked him to her office.

At her grim expression, his stomach had twisted. The situation reminded him too much of the times people had brought him news of a loss.

"Please have a seat, my Lord," Nellie said once they were in her office.

"I think I would prefer to stand."

"No, my Lord. *Sit.*" She pointed to the chair in front of her desk, and he did as she said.

"Has she gone?" His words came out tight and low, almost a growl.

"Yes. I'm so sorry, my Lord."

Gareth's rigid shoulders slumped, the weight of the news too heavy to bear, and he leaned back in the chair. It was too much like that day when he'd lost Cecily. This time, he felt as though he were looking down upon himself, unable to rage as he'd done then. How was it that he was still able to sit upright?

"She left you a letter, my Lord."

Numbly, he looked up. Aunt Nellie held an unsealed envelope. Had she opened it? He couldn't bring himself to care if she'd read it before he had. When she held it closer to him, he finally reached out to accept it. His fingers tingled with magic where they touched the envelope. Was it residue of the same dust that had sent Catherine away from him?

He stared at the letter. Did he want to know what she'd written? Did he care? It would change nothing. Cecily and his son had been ripped from his life. Catherine had chosen to leave him.

She was gone, and he was dead. Dead. Dead.

"My Lord, please." Aunt Nellie had come around the desk and taken the chair beside his. "Read it." When he didn't move, she gently took the envelope from his unresisting fingers and removed the letter. Once she'd opened the folds, she put it in his hand again.

My dearest Gareth,

I had an epiphany this afternoon. All this time I've worried about what I *would be giving up if I stayed in your time. It was selfish of me, but it was also the truth, so there you have it. I cannot survive if I'm not actively trying to heal people. I've been this way since I was a little girl.*

This afternoon you showed me something I admire in you—your kind heart and your willingness to learn. I saw all your hard work and the lives that will be made better because you can be their advocate.

I also saw what a future with me—were I to be true to myself—would mean for you. The people of your station would never accept a female doctor. You would become a social pariah, and your ability to champion good causes would be taken from you.

One of my basic tenents as a doctor is that I must do no harm. I love you too much to do that to you.

Catherine

Gareth stared at the words, at first unable to take them in. *I love you too much.* She loved him too much to stay with him.

He had no idea how long he sat with the letter in his lap.

"My lord, the magic tells me this is not over, so please do not despair." Aunt Nellie took back the letter and folded it again before placing it in the envelope. "I will get you a cup of tea—"

"None of your faerie tricks." Gareth slowly stood, his body aching like that of an old man.

"Please, my Lord."

"I'm done with magic." He left the room. His people, at least, needed him.

Present Day

Aunt Nellie had arrived with her recovery potion, and Lulu had found some modern clothes for Catherine since her other outfit had been covered in blood. They gave her back her old ones in a plastic bag in case she needed them when the police questioned her.

As she prepared to step into a different Twickenham vehicle, Aunt Nellie approached her.

"My dear, I know you're hurting, but I want you to understand that this is not finished."

"It better be because I can't take any more." Catherine reaffirmed her decision to never return to Twickenham Manor.

Walter was silent during the drive to her flat.

"Thank you," she said as she got out. "For everything." She didn't look back as she went inside her apartment building.

She stood in the doorway of her flat and stared at her living room. The last time she'd been there had been the morning of the terrorist attack. Yesterday. The room felt alien, no longer belonging to her.

Catherine sank to a chair and called the authorities. She apologized for the delay in contacting them, saying she must have been suffering from PTSD when she wandered off in shock.

They were particularly interested in the whereabouts of the man Catherine had entered the restaurant with. She reported that she only knew that his name was Gareth and they'd just met recently and done some sightseeing together. No, she didn't have a way to contact him.

When she returned to work two days later, her supervisor had started to chide Catherine for having left the scene, but after looking closely at her had suggested she should take the rest of her holiday time off. She chose to go back to work instead and even picked up extra shifts. It felt a lot like after her family had been killed.

Every night she fell into an exhausted sleep. It didn't keep her from dreaming about Gareth. The pain in her chest never went away, only lessened to a dull ache. She was used to loss though and, after a while, she knew she'd eventually almost forget it. Almost. Except when she'd find herself rubbing the spot over her heart.

20

GARETH DROVE HIMSELF INTO HIS estate business. Only when Ellen wanted to participate in a social event did he bother to go out. The only place he refused to escort her to was Twickenham.

She'd only remarked on his behavior once, and he'd snapped at her. He'd apologized immediately, but she hadn't asked again. Sometimes, in the evenings when they would sit together after dinner—her pouring over seed catalogs and he working on the estate's books— he would catch her watching him, her expression worried. There was nothing he could do to allay her concerns for him.

It seemed strangely quiet now with just the two of them. Before his sister had befriended Reese and changed their lives, he would frequently have guests stay at Kellworth, and Ellen's companion would always sit with them in the evenings. When the woman had chosen to stay on to help with her sister's new baby, Ellen had decided not to replace her.

Grandmama was now established in the dower house. The two women had already begun planning for Ellen's season. He meant to make sure his sister did not feel pressured to make a match she did not want. If she did choose to marry, she would move to her own home, and he would be truly alone.

Gareth would miss her terribly. Without her to push him to attend social events, he would likely turn into a recluse. For the sake of those he wished to help, he mustn't allow that to happen. There were things he could do, power he could wield, in the House of Lords. If he faded into obscurity, he would be useless to his people.

He'd begun meeting with his new man of business and his tenants. Ellen had insisted on attending as well. She'd said that Reese had first found it necessary to assess what skills and tools the women in the village had before she could determine what they needed. His sister had said it would work for this as well, and she'd been correct.

"Gareth," Ellen said at breakfast one morning in October, "we have an invitation to wedding festivities at Twickenham."

He didn't bother to look up from the newspaper he was reading as he ate. He had no intention of going to Twickenham. It held too many memories. When she'd asked him to take her to the September ball there, he'd flatly refused. Grandmama had escorted her, and Ellen had said the old woman had complained the entire time.

"But this is a special invitation from the *duke of Hertfordshire*."

"Simon is getting married?" Gareth asked, surprised enough to look up.

"He's marrying Cora Rey."

She said the name as though it should mean something to him. Gareth took a bite of his food. It did sound vaguely familiar. Who was this Cora Rey? The image of a pretty blonde woman standing next to a Twickenham portrait of five people came to mind. He choked on his food and started coughing.

"*Reese's* American friend is marrying Simon?" he asked when he could speak.

"Yes, and I find it delightfully romantic." She gave her brother a shrewd look. "I wonder if her friends will attend."

Gareth sat up straighter and drank from his glass. He would love to see Reese again and verify that Taylor was making her happy.

"I thought that might get your attention," Ellen said, smiling now. "We must show Reese the village while she's here. She might have further recommendations, especially about that property you're looking at for your school."

"Yes, indeed."

"So, you will attend?" she asked slyly.

"Yes, you minx. I will attend."

GARETH GLANCED at Ellen as the carriage approached Twickenham Manor. She'd been as edgy about the upcoming meeting as he. The actual wedding was a small, private affair that would be celebrated with the others attending Aunt Nellie's Full Moon Ball.

"I didn't realize Sir Jack Hughes would be in attendance," Gareth said when he recognized the baron's carriage.

"Yes. He was on good terms with Mr. Taylor's sister."

Gareth helped Ellen from their carriage and escorted her into the manor. He scanned the room, hoping to see Reese. Sir Jack stood nearby with his cousin Amelia, greeting a few familiar-looking people.

"Speaking of Mr. Taylor's sister, there she is with Sir Hughes," Ellen whispered.

"Then Reese should have come as well."

His sister craned her neck, searching the crush of people. And then Gareth saw Reese. Ellen gave a little squeal and ran forward, completely forgetting her manners. The two women threw their arms around each other, crying. He smiled for the first time in weeks.

When he glanced at Jem, he found the man watching him, a crease between his brows. Gareth strode over and extended his hand.

"It is good to see you again, Mr. Taylor. I must say that you and Reese look extremely happy."

"We are, and please call me Jem, my Lord," he said. "I'm well, but I have to say that you look terrible. You look like you've lost weight. Have you been sick?"

"Ah," Aunt Nellie said, taking them each by the arm and trying to nudge them toward her office, "I am so happy to see you both on such good terms."

"No, please," Gareth said, gently but firmly pulling his arm free. "I have no wish to be reminded of my last visit to your office. We are here to offer our congratulations to the happy couple and see old friends. That is all."

Aunt Nellie let out an irritated sigh and took his arm again. Rather than create a scene, Gareth allowed her to tow him to her office, but he stayed by the door.

"I feel your pain, your Lordship," Jem said, studying the office. "Did you get lectured in here too?"

"Indeed," Gareth said. "I would like to give my regards to Reese and then be gone."

"I told you, my Lord, that you must work *with* the magic." Aunt Nellie gestured for him to take a seat. "Hiding away at Kellworth is not the way to do that."

"And I told you I'm finished with magic."

"I think I'm missing something." Jem glanced first at one and then the other. "This isn't about me and Reese, is it?"

"No. His Lordship made a trip to your time last August."

"That *was* you in that video then," Jem exclaimed. "Reese was sure it was, but I convinced her it couldn't be. Oh man," he gasped. "Then you know Catherine."

"How do you know her?" Gareth stalked toward the American, his jaw tight.

"Whoa. Hang on there," Jem said, backing up, his hands held defensively before him. "I danced with her at Nellie's ball before we were first zapped here, and then she happened to be nearby when we came down the stairs after. *Oh*. This is about you and her, isn't it?"

Gareth turned and strode from the room.

"What did I say?" Jem asked as Gareth was closing the door.

The noise from the ballroom blocked Nellie's response. He entered the room and searched for his sister, assuming she would be with Reese. She was. By the time he reached them, he hoped he had his composure back. Ellen would be sure to question him if he had not.

Reese saw him first. Her face lit up, and she came to him with both hands extended. Gareth took them and bowed while she curtsied. He'd forgotten how tall she was. When he turned her left hand, he found a simple wedding band.

"You look happy, Mrs. Taylor."

"I am, my Lord. Very much."

"I am happy for you." There was that at least. "May I have the next dance?"

"Of course."

Fortunately, when the music began, it was a waltz, making it easier to talk. Reese bubbled with excitement about all his sister had told her about the village.

"We have some ideas for future ventures and would appreciate your thoughts," he said. "Would you be willing to make a visit to the village tomorrow?"

"Ellen already asked me. We'd love to come." Reese's voice turned serious. "Are you all right, Gareth? You've got dark circles under your eyes."

"It has been a difficult few months but for reasons other than you may think. Please do not blame yourself for my situation. My sister and the memory of your friendship have given me strength." There was so much he would like to tell her, but he hadn't even been able to speak of it to Ellen.

"I hope so."

When the dance ended, he escorted her to her husband. From his expression, Gareth knew Aunt Nellie had played the gabster. How had that woman managed to keep her fae secret if she had no more discretion than that?

"I will pay my respects to their Graces," he said, "and then I will return to Kellworth."

"Already?" Reese asked, disappointed.

Gareth glanced around the room. "I would prefer not to be here." He caught Jem's sympathetic gaze. Gareth clenched his fists. His emotions were too near the surface here. "I look forward to tomorrow. Ellen will be staying the night." He bowed and strode away.

THE VISIT to his tenant village turned into a fortnight-long visit at Kellworth. Their guests showed Gareth how much he had been neglecting Ellen in his morose state. For her sake, he promised himself to do better.

Reese and Jem both made excellent suggestions for additional improvements to the tenant village. She commented that with such an industrious group of residents, it might become a center for cottage industries, where businesses were conducted out of homes. He liked the idea of his tenants being so capable, and it drove home how much they would need additional training on how to run a business.

The four of them made the drive to the farm adjacent to his estate that he had considered purchasing.

"And what do you have in mind for this?" Jem asked as the ladies rode ahead toward the large farmhouse.

"I have thought it could be a place of learning. Reese spoke often of 'life skills' and how many of my cottiers didn't have them."

"A school for adults?" Jem nodded thoughtfully. "I like it. That's just the kind of stuff she's doing at home."

"Yes. That was what inspired me to build a school where adults could be taught. I believe the surrounding farmland should bring in enough to maintain the school. The teacher could live here and the students come for lessons."

"I like it too," Reese said. She and Ellen had brought their horses to a stop so the men could catch up to them. "You'll need to be flexible and willing to try new things until you find a system that works."

"Must you return to America?" Ellen asked wistfully. "Would this not be a perfect place for you? This is what you do at your home. Why not perform the same work here?"

"Oh Ellen." Reese reached over and squeezed her hand. "Don't tempt me. We both have families we couldn't leave, and they wouldn't want to come here. But, there's going to be a Christmas ball in December as part of the wedding festivities. We're going to see if we can make it back for that."

"I don't understand how you are able to make the journey again so soon." Ellen frowned. "Does it not take weeks to sail to America?"

"They have some faster ships. Jem has a family friend in the shipping business with one of them." Reese glanced away from Ellen and met Gareth's gaze. She widened her eyes and pulled a face, showing she didn't like lying to his sister.

Jem asked Ellen a question, and they rode ahead with her pointing toward something near the house.

"Now if we can just figure out how to help you," Reese said softly.

Gareth shook his head. Nothing could be done to help him.

"You were pretty amazing in that video," she said.

"I don't wish to speak of it."

"Gareth." Reese's voice was still low but had taken on a sharp quality he was all too familiar with from her first visit. "Why are you taking this lying down? Wasn't that you who came bursting in when we were about to leave because you wanted to make sure I'd be happy?"

He refused to answer.

"Aunt Nellie told me what the letter said."

Gareth growled. "That bothersome woman. It is none of her concern."

"But she's queen of the magic. Jem and I both fought against it. We were wrong. Nellie keeps saying you have to work *with* the magic. It sounds like you and Catherine were in a bad place when she left. Have you considered that you might be letting her go too easily?"

"*She* left. I will not disrespect her decision."

"I'll bet she really did leave because she thought it was best for you, but what if what she really needs is for you to come after her? You checked up on me. Why haven't you checked to make sure she's all right too?"

His pulse quickened. Reese's words spoke truth to his heart, and he felt an odd tingle, like the one when the magic powder touched him. Was it trying to communicate with him? Should he listen to it?

"Two smart people who love each other as much as you two do ought to be able to find a way to make it work, Gareth. Think about it."

CHAPTER 21

PRESENT DAY

CATHERINE HAD FINALLY SLIPPED INTO a routine with a semblance of the one she'd had before Gareth. She couldn't keep up the same work schedule forever, or so her supervisor had said, so she was looking ahead for how to use the time off over the holidays, someplace not full of memories of him.

As she turned the corner onto the street where she lived, she noticed a Twickenham car sitting outside her building. Her stomach knotted, and she was about to turn back the way she'd come when the door opened and a very tall and familiar-looking woman jumped out.

"Don't go, Catherine."

She recognized the woman now from her portrait. Reese. The other door had opened and Jem Taylor stepped out. Seeing them made it all real again, brought pain to the front, and Catherine had to blink at the sudden stinging in her eyes.

"I know who you are," she said when she could speak. "Why are you here?"

"We'd like to talk to you if you'll let us," he said.

"Is there somewhere close we could get a bite to eat and chat?" Reese asked.

"Our treat," Jem added.

Too many memories came flooding in. Why did they have to come and ruin the balance she'd worked so hard to find?

"Please," Reese said, her tone charged with emotion, like she was worried for someone.

Was it Gareth? Sudden worry made the ache in Catherine's chest sharpen to a pain.

"There's a place around the corner that has good fish and chips," she said.

"Thank you." Jem brought his hands together like he was praying and gave a little bow.

"You want us to call you to come get us when we're done, Walter?" Reese asked the driver.

"I'm fine here, Mrs. Taylor."

"This way." Catherine pointed to the street where she and Gareth had always begun their days.

The Taylors joined her so they walked abreast. Someone was handing out fliers, and she accepted one. It was for a Victorian Christmas Festival the last week of November. Just what she needed, a reminder of something Victorian. Catherine shoved it into her purse.

Since it was a little early for supper, the little restaurant wasn't very full yet. No one said anything until they were seated and had placed their orders.

"I thought you'd gone back to the States," Catherine said when the waiter had gone.

"We had, but we returned for a wedding."

Had they come to tell Catherine that Gareth had married someone else? The thought of him with another woman else made her body burn with jealousy. She stamped it down. It stupid and unfair to him. She should be happy for him if he had.

"No, it's not Gareth. I'm sorry." Reese reached across the table and grasped Catherine's hand. "My old roommate, one of the people who traveled in time with us, married a duke back then."

Catherine allowed herself to breathe again. She was angry at her reaction. With difficulty, she reminded herself that Gareth finding someone in his own time to marry would be a good thing.

For everyone but her. She pushed the thought aside.

"We did see his Lordship though," Jem said.

Catherine forced her expression to remain neutral, but her hand twitched under Reese's. Her modern-day friend had stayed to marry a duke? No. Catherine wouldn't think about it.

"He's not doing well." Reese's expression had gone from sympathetic to worried. "Ellen—you've met his sister, right? She says he's closed himself off from most social functions, and she's worried he may not go to London during the Season even for Parliament."

"He can't do that," Catherine cried. "He needs to be there to push his agenda. That's why I left, so he could carry on his work. His people need him."

"Everyone handles grief differently," Jem said. "He might come around, but then he might not."

"Well, that was a totally worthless comment, Jem Taylor." Reese rolled her eyes but then gave him a quick kiss.

"If I can't say anything encouraging," he said in a voice very much like that of Bambi's little rabbit friend, "I shouldn't say anything at all."

The waiter chose then to bring their food, so they put the conversation on hold. The Taylors each took a bite and then grinned at each other.

"This is so good," Jem said.

"I think it's the best I've had anywhere in London," Reese added.

Catherine stared at her food, having no appetite. Why was Gareth doing this? She'd made sure he could continue to help his people.

"I have a question for you," Reese said.

Catherine glanced at the woman but didn't say anything.

"If he came to you and asked if you two could figure out a way to make it work, would you consider it?"

"Do you love him enough to try?" Jem added in a soft voice.

"How dare you," Catherine hissed, her heart hurting like the knife in it had been given a twist. "You know nothing about me."

Reese had frowned at her husband's question but then bristled at the criticism. She pinched her lips and took a deep breath before speaking.

"We didn't mean to offend. Gareth is a dear friend, and we only want him to be happy. I'm going to ask you the same thing I asked him."

"Please don't." Catherine closed her eyes against the stinging.

"Wouldn't two intelligent people who are deeply in love be able to find a way to work the system so they can be together?"

Reese squeezed her hand, and Catherine felt an odd tingle like whenever Aunt Nellie had used the magic dust stuff. Catherine opened her eyes.

"Just think about it." Reese signaled the waiter for the check. "We'll be back in a couple of months. I hope to find you happier."

Still angry, Catherine watched them leave. It was ridiculous. How could she be a doctor in his time? No. She wouldn't think about it and set herself up for more heartbreak. She left her food uneaten and walked back to her flat.

Telling herself not to think about Gareth only worked when she was awake. After seven nights in a row dreaming about him, Catherine was exhausted. She sat on the edge of her bed on the eighth night and stared at her reflection in the glass door on her closet. No wonder coworkers kept asking her if she was sick.

With a sigh, she surrendered. She didn't have enough energy to fight against thoughts of him. As much as it hurt, she felt a little peace for the first time. She hadn't come up with any solutions, but she no longer felt like she was at war with herself.

When Catherine cleaned out her purse a couple of weeks later, she found the flier about the Victorian Christmas Festival that would kick off the season. It appeared that all the businesses in a three-block radius had been invited to participate. That explained some of the stores she'd noticed that were now carrying Victorian-style clothing and accessories.

For one weekend, they would close off the street nearest hers to vehicles. It would be a festival, with street performers from the period, braziers to keep warm, crafts for children, and food vendors. All the shops and restaurants would be open and people were encouraged to come in costume. It sounded like fun, and she needed to get out if only to remind herself that she was alive.

She broke down and called Nellie about the possibility of borrowing one of the gowns from the period. Walter showed up a couple of days later with the same dress she'd worn to 1850 and a lovely matching cloak.

"Seriously?" Catherine gave Walter a flat look and said, "Leave it to Nellie to send a message."

He then handed her an envelope. It had her name scrawled on it in masculine writing. Her hands started to shake, and Walter covered them with his.

"I've lived a very long time, doctor, and I cannot tell you the number of people I've seen turn their back on happiness because they're afraid. Some feared being hurt and some of hurting others. *I* say, don't be afraid of something so right." He dropped his hands and nodded sagely. "I've seen that video. Neither you nor his Lordship are cowards, so I believe you should stop acting like one." Walter then returned to the car and drove away.

Catherine couldn't bring herself to open the envelope, so she put it in the cloak's pocket and hung up the clothing. She'd worry about them when she had to.

CATHERINE HAD to work the first day of the Victorian Christmas Festival. It had been a crazy day at the A&E and had included her kneeling on the concrete outside of a car, essentially catching the baby who'd refused to wait until his mother could get inside. It was always such a rush to deliver a baby.

Catherine handed off the newborn to nursery staff, her thoughts going to Gareth. Had they let him see his son? Would his wife have died if she'd given birth in modern times? While obstetrics wasn't Catherine's specialty, she'd been curious and checked out the statistics. Women did still die in or following childbirth, but the numbers were per hundred thousand rather than per thousand as they had been in 1850.

When she made her way home, she thought she'd be too tired to attend the festival, but she found that the delivery had exhilarated her. No surprise that. Every time she'd had an opportunity to deliver a baby, it'd made her wonder if she'd chosen the wrong specialty.

After she'd showered, she opened the closet and examined the beautiful dress Nellie had sent over. Catherine missed Gareth so much. But she was going to think about the street party and not the charming earl, otherwise she might cry, and then she definitely wouldn't go out. She really needed to.

When she turned the dress around, she found that Nellie's people had changed out the bazillion buttons in the back with a zipper. Bless her!

Catherine was surprised at how quickly she remembered the process of dressing for the period. Because she hadn't had time to have her hair done, she pulled it back in a simple bun. She'd have on a bonnet anyway.

She pulled the cloak from its hanger, and something dropped to the floor. The envelope Walter had brought her. She hadn't been able to bring herself to open it.

Heaving out a breath, she bent to pick it up. She ran her fingers over her name, imagining Gareth sitting at a desk, quill in hand. While she'd never seen his writing, she was sure it was his. It fit. Curious, she lifted it to her nose and inhaled.

An explosion of memories assaulted her. Choosing pastries from her favorite shop. Gareth's childlike fascination with every little trinket in the stores. His expression when she'd used the Oyster Card for the Tube. His fear on the Eye, and the feel of his shoulder against her cheek. The way he'd stepped between her and a madman with a knife.

Catherine rubbed her chest. How she loved that man.

Walter's parting words came to her. They'd been good words, but he was wrong. She *was* a coward. Every night since the visit by the two Americans, she'd dreamed of Gareth. Each night he'd looked progressively worse, no longer the robust man in the peak of health. The dreams were doubly unsettling because she couldn't decide if they represented the Gareth that Reese had described or the one destroyed by his connection with Catherine.

She stilled. His connection with *her*. He had that already, and there was nothing they could do about it. Was the haggard man, aged beyond his years, his future regardless of what she chose? Had she doomed him the first time she'd stepped into that portrait room and seen his picture?

No. She didn't believe in fate, refused to believe in it. *Nothing* had the power to decide her future except *her*.

Catherine's heart lurched. And Gareth. She felt queasy. He was a part of this, and she'd taken away his right to have a say. She turned over the letter and looked at the wax seal. The intricate letter "H" was beautifully intertwined with what looked like an outline of the letter "K." For Kellworth?

She retrieved her letter opener and sliced the end so she could preserve the beautiful seal. Taking a deep breath, she slid out the letter and opened it.

My dearest Catherine,

I have made an honest attempt to set aside my own desires and honor your wishes. A dear friend questioned the wisdom of that decision, and I find I have come to agree that it is the wrong one.

In your letter, you expressed your love for me. Over these weeks, I have held that dear. Upon reflection, I do not know why you and I cannot find a way for us to be together and still meet our obligations, both to ourselves and to others.

Aunt Nellie has told me of a festival you plan to attend. I would brave your world of mad assassins so I may escort you.

All my love,

Gareth

Was he here? Catherine's hands shook as she grabbed her skirts and ran to the window. Below, at the entrance to her building, was a man dressed in exquisite Victorian attire, including a knee-length overcoat and top hat. Her heart gave a painful jump at the familiar stride as he walked back and forth.

Gareth.

For a second her knees went weak. He was *here*. She ran back to the closet and grabbed the cloak and hat. It took three tries before she could get the bow tied for her bonnet. She made sure her reticule held her phone, wallet, and keys before dashing out the door. The elevator took forever, so she used the stairs and was a little breathless as she approached the door to the outside.

When Catherine opened it, Gareth spun around. Their gazes met, and she experienced a delicious kind of pain. For the first time, she completely understood what Elizabeth Bennett must have felt when Mr. Darcy had appeared at her house when she thought she'd lost him.

Catherine wanted to throw herself in his arms, but an unexpected shyness held her back. Gareth watched her, wary, and a hesitant twitch tugged at the corner of his mouth. She smiled, and his whole body seemed to relax. He bowed. She curtsied and went down the steps, extending her hand.

"Your Lordship," she said as he took it and pressed it to his lips.

She wished she hadn't already put on her gloves. "You look better than I was led to believe you would."

"The rumors of my decline, while true, were grossly exaggerated." He slid her arm through his and nodded toward the T-intersection and one of the streets where the festival was being held. "Shall we go?"

What she wanted to do was drag him up to her apartment and kiss him silly. Her breathing hitched at the thought, and her hand twitched.

"Are you unwell?" He dropped her arm and turned to study her, full of the concern that was so Gareth.

It made her feel treasured and, oddly, empowered. Reese had been right. Catherine had given up on them too easily. Her heart told her that with this man, almost any obstacle could be overcome.

Catherine reached up and cupped his cheeks. "I love you, Gareth Hildebrand, and I want you in my future even if it's in the past."

"My *love*." He crushed her to him and pressed his lips to hers.

Her hands moved around his neck and then into his hair, knocking his hat to the ground. She kissed his mouth, his cheeks, and then his mouth again. His chest rumbled and he pulled her closer, kissing her until they were both breathing raggedly.

"Please tell me you'll marry me," he finally huffed. "I cannot survive without you."

"I—" Catherine wanted this, wanted *him*. They had to figure out how to make this work.

"Must you work in a hospital?" Gareth's voice had taken on a panicked edge to it. "Could you not teach midwives? I promise to assist you in every way possible. Should anyone question why a lady of quality would do so, the history of my late wife's death should be answer enough of why I would encourage and support your endeavors."

Catherine's thoughts went back to when she'd delivered the

baby and her theory that Cecily and their son might have been saved if someone had been there with modern knowledge. A sense of rightness filled Catherine for the first time since she'd first laid eyes on Gareth's portrait. But would she be able to learn enough to fit into his station and be a help to *his* efforts?

"But what if I don't fit in with the aristocracy?"

"Oh, my darling, you were able to complete rigorous training to become a physician. I have seen you in the most trying of circumstances. I have no doubts in your ability to learn the rules of my society."

Catherine met Gareth's tender, pleading gaze. Now that she'd seen him, held him, she knew she couldn't let him go again. With that realization, the darkness that had been her constant companion for three months disappeared, the pain bursting from her chest like it'd been overcome by the light of Aunt Nellie's faerie magic. In its place, she felt peace and a sense of rightness.

"Yes, Gareth, I'll marry you."

His face lit up. He kissed her again, and Catherine lost herself in his nearness, his masculine scent, the feel of his arms about her, the heat of his mouth on hers.

"Marry me when we return," Gareth said when they finally came up for breath. "Aunt Nellie told me the full moon in your time will be on December twenty-second but on the nineteenth in 1850. Upon my return, I will drive immediately to London to obtain a special license, and we can be wed at Kellworth—or Twickenham if you prefer." Gareth frowned. "Unless your heart is set on a grand ceremony."

"No. Small and simple works for me." Catherine cupped his cheeks, unable to stop touching him, to prove to herself he was really there.

"Then we shall do it that way." Gareth pressed his lips to hers again. "The duke of Hertfordshire is hosting a Christmas ball, and I wish to attend so I may introduce you to everyone as my countess. We will have less than a month here. Is that sufficient time for you to make arrangements with your hospital and to sever the lease for your lodging?"

A thrill of excitement ran through Catherine, and she shivered as the reality of her decision struck her.

"Are you cold?" Gareth started to unbutton his overcoat like he meant to give it to her.

"No, I'm fine." She redid the buttons, saying, "This is going to be a really big change for me."

"Are you having doubts?" he asked, covering her hands with his.

"No, Gareth." Catherine smiled as that sense of peace and rightness strengthened inside her. She pressed her lips to his. "I'm more than fine. Now, let's stop making a spectacle of ourselves. I want you to check out all this Victorian Christmas stuff, and you can tell me if they got any of it right."

EPILOGUE

"THAT'S THE PERFECT COLOR FOR your eyes," Catherine said as she fluffed out the skirt to Ellen's newest gown.

"Just as I said it would." Grandmama Hildebrand shifted her massive body in the chair, and it groaned.

Catherine and Ellen exchanged alarmed glances, but the chair didn't fall apart. Gareth was going to have to put pressure on that furniture-maker to finish the new one ASAP. Catherine had tried unsuccessfully to get Grandmama to cut back on her portion sizes, but the old woman would have none of it. Catherine thought back to the first time she had attempted the conversation.

"I only have one thing to look forward to in my days, and that's my food." Grandmama had glared at Catherine and Gareth before waving them away. "A newlywed couple like you shouldn't be wasting your time visiting an old woman. Go home and make babies for me to spoil."

They'd barely made it out of the dower house before bursting into laughter.

"I'm so sorry," Gareth had said when he could speak. "She's gotten far worse as she's aged. She used to have *some* discretion."

"Plain spoken just like my grandmother was." Catherine had then pulled him to her by his cravat and kissed him. "But Grand-mama had a *very* good suggestion."

"She did indeed." He had hurriedly helped her into the curricle for the return trip home.

Smiling at the memory, Catherine's hand automatically went to her abdomen. She wasn't showing yet. It still surprised her that she could be so happy, considering how difficult the decision had been to come with Gareth.

"Are you unwell?" Ellen asked.

"Never better." Catherine picked up her notepad. "What's next on the list?"

"I hope that someday I find a man who will make me as happy as Gareth does you," Ellen said with a sigh.

"You make too much of your brother's love matches," Grand-mama said in disgust. "In my day, we let our parents choose for us. Love had nothing to do with the decision."

"I thought you never married." Catherine turned to face the woman, her curiosity-itch coming alive for the first time in months. "I heard Colonel Pritchard say you were quite the beauty in your day."

"That's a faradiddle, but I would expect nothing less from that old codger." Grandmama's cheeks had flushed at the compliment, and her voice turned sad. "He used to trail after me at every social event, until he was sent to India. He was the youngest son, so Papa didn't approve of him."

Catherine glanced at Ellen, who shrugged. Was that why the old woman had never married; her love had been sent to India, and she'd chosen not to go against her parents to follow him? Was this what Catherine would have been like if she hadn't chosen to come with Gareth, a grizzled old A&E doctor with no life?

The sound of a carriage outside pulled her from her thoughts, and she hurried to the door.

"You must not act like that yourself, Ellen," Grandmama said.

"It's unseemly for two people to fawn over each other as those two do in public."

"But that's what I want for myself, Grandmama."

When Catherine opened the door, Gareth was handing the reins to his groom.

"Well, are you ladies satisfied with the dressmaker's work?" He pulled her in for a kiss before she could reply.

"We can't do this in London," she said when she could speak. "Grandmama says it's vulgar. I think she's jealous."

"She is correct about how the Ton would see it. I have no wish to embarrass my sister. That's why I plan to take advantage of it while I can." Gareth kissed her again.

"Will you two stop that and come inside before I freeze to death?" Grandmama grumbled.

Chuckling, he took Catherine's hand and they went into the dower house.

"Did you have any luck with the Colonel?" Ellen asked when they'd gathered around the tea tray.

"I don't understand all these changes you're proposing." Grandmama's tone was querulous, but her irritation hadn't impacted her appetite.

Catherine watched surreptitiously as the old woman took a bite of cake. After having a little chat with the dower house cook, Catherine had managed to convince the woman to try a small change to the recipe. Just a *little* less sugar to start with. The goal was to slowly bring down Grandmama's taste for sweets.

Gareth gave a little nod that he'd also noticed the success of the first step. Now they only needed to keep her alive while they tried to improve her health.

"I've explained it to you already, Grandmama," he said. "It is part of a progressive business plan to increase the estate's annual revenues."

"But a school for adults? How will giving them time away from farming your land increase your coffers?"

"With more knowledge, the quality of their work will improve," Ellen said. "Would you like more tea, Catherine?"

"I'm good."

She didn't mention the health clinic they planned to add to the old house. They were trying to be subtle about her part in that. She'd met with a couple of the midwives who serviced the Kellworth tenants to observe their practices. Her modern sensibilities had been both appalled and impressed. Considering what little scientific knowledge they had, they'd shown themselves innovative. The important thing to Catherine was that they all wanted the same outcome: healthy babies and mothers.

"I'm worried that I won't find someone who is of a like mind," Ellen said, pulling Catherine from her reverie.

From the few social events they'd attended since their marriage, she shared the girl's worries. What Ellen needed was a man with a modern viewpoint, and Catherine doubted there'd be many of those among the Ton. When people had plenty of money, it was hard to convince them to change.

She glanced at Gareth, grateful again that she'd found one who could. Ellen mustn't end up like Grandmama because of society's limitations.

There had to be someone out there for the girl. The Season would run until August, though Catherine hoped they wouldn't have to stay there that long. She was due in September and didn't want to risk not being able to get to Twickenham in time to go back to the future for the delivery.

She moved her hand to her abdomen again and glanced at her husband. He was watching her and covered her hand with his.

"What's this?" Grandmama asked, suddenly excited. "Are you increasing?"

Catherine smiled. Oh yes. She was increasing in so many more ways than the rotund woman could imagine.

I HOPE you enjoyed Gareth and Catherine's love story. But this doesn't end the Twickenham saga, so don't leave yet. Ellen's love story is yet to come. If you'd like to find out more about Reese's time travel adventure, on the next page is the first chapter of *Against the Magic*, And don't forget Ellen's love story!

Leave a review for *With the Magic* now!

Get a free book by joining Donna K. Weaver's Reader Group and hear all the great news about new releases and sales. Type in the following: https://landing.mailerlite.com/webforms/landing/t1k1v8

After reading the beginning of *With the Magic*, turn the page to read the first chapter of *For the Magic*, Ellen's love story.

CHAPTER 1: AGAINST THE MAGIC

PRESENT DAY

JEM TAYLOR FIGURED THIS TRIP home would either result in smooth sailing or swift sinking. He'd messed up rather spectacularly with Reese two years ago, so he expected the latter. Following the advice of his grandmother who'd always encouraged him to pursue his dreams, he'd decided to take her at her words: Nothing ventured, nothing gained.

Too bad gran hadn't mentioned a sick feeling in the gut while out doing that venturing. But, he needed to see his family first and then seek out Reese.

Taking a deep breath, Jem strode toward the front porch. He didn't recognize the SUV in the driveway. Either his dad or his sister Kaitlyn had a new car. Jem had barely put his foot on the top porch step when a squeal rang through the open window.

"Jem!" his sister's voice shouted. "Mom, it's Jem."

The door burst open, and Kaitlyn launched herself into his arms. As he returned her embrace, he found himself at the center of a skirmish as his parents joined her in what could only be called a giant group hug. Finally, his mother stepped back, wiping her eyes.

"Jamison Taylor, why didn't you tell us you were coming?" she asked.

"Why didn't you come two days ago?" Kaitlyn asked, her tone accusatory. "*I* came to *your* graduation, but *you* couldn't make it to *mine?*"

"Give him room to breathe," their father said. "You'll make it so he never wants to come home again."

He let them pull him into the house, knowing that he'd have to put up with the fussing before they would let him get a word in.

"Well, let's get him inside." His mother looked him up and down while tugging on his arm. "Didn't they feed you on that Broadway play?"

His mother pestered Jem with questions but then never gave him a chance to answer any of them. His father took Jem's back-pack and set it down near the stairs to be taken up later. He smothered a grin, having forgotten about his father's reputation for economy of movement. No point in making unnecessary trips up the stairs.

Kaitlyn and his mother went to the kitchen to work on the last preparations of the evening meal and left him to help his father set the table.

"Your sister has a point, you know," his father finally said. "Why couldn't you make it?"

"Didn't Kate tell you? I sent her a text explaining. The other stage manager had an emergency appendectomy. I couldn't get away." Jem straightened the fork by the china plate. "I did want to be here. You know how tricky it can get to take time off during a run. That's why I never promised to come."

"I guess." His father's tone still carried disapproval.

Jem had already fought this battle and had no intention of being drawn into it again. If he hadn't managed to get the attention of a retired local celebrity and garnered a scholarship, Jem would have had to pay for his four years of theater school himself. His father had refused to help. The decision to go on the road with a traveling Broadway play had nearly given the old man a stroke.

His father eyed him up and down, considering. "Even though we've talked every few days online, you look different in person. Older. More mature. You going out on tour again?"

"I haven't decided yet." Jem folded a napkin the way his mother liked them and placed it under the fork. "The director has a new project starting in the fall, and she said she's interested in working with me again as her stage manager. I just don't know if I want to be on the road for so long."

"Your mother hates you being gone all the time, you know." His father's expression said that he agreed with his wife's sentiments on the matter.

"Honey, can you come finish the platter?" Jem's mother called.

His father left the table, and Kaitlyn came to take his place.

"Did I hear that right?" she asked. "You might go out *again*?"

"Not from you too," Jem said, already weary. Why didn't they realize he had to do what was best to further his career?

"Please don't go away again." Kaitlyn tugged at his arm and took on the little-girl whiny voice she'd used as a child, but the twinkle in her eyes told him she was teasing. "Mom missed you. Dad missed you. Even *I* missed you."

A surge of affection for his teasing, irritating, charming little sister filled him, and Jem pulled her into a hug. She didn't hesitate to encircle his waist with her arms. "I've missed you too, kiddo." He pulled back and glanced down at her. "You know I did want to come to your graduation, right?"

"Well, I know the other stage manager didn't rupture his appendix just to ruin my graduation experience." The whining in Kaitlyn's voice sounded real this time when she said, "I don't know why you're always so closed-mouthed about your travel plans, always showing up at the last minute. Without any notice. Even the one Christmas you made it here, we had no idea you were coming until you showed up at the door."

"You know how Mom is." Jem kept his voice low, his eyes darting to where his mother stood tossing a salad. "I didn't want to set her up for disappointment if I couldn't get away. Better to let it be a surprise."

"All it did was drive us crazy," Kaitlyn whispered. "Can't you find work closer to home?"

"This is ready," Mother said as she came out of the kitchen. "I hope you have a good appetite, Jem, because I'm going to fatten you up while you're here." She scrutinized him with a hard glare. "And how long might that be this time?"

"Let's sit down, and we can talk about it over dinner." His father put the platter with the meat, carrots, and potatoes beside the salad and other side dishes.

They spent the next hour getting updated since the last time they had talked online. Whenever his mother pressed Jem for an answer about how long he planned to stay, he redirected the discussion. He knew she was letting him do it, but both Kaitlyn and his father pinched their lips every time he did.

Jem didn't know what to tell them. A part of him knew it would be a great thing for his career to work with this director again. She was going places, and he had no doubt that it wouldn't take long before she was on Broadway rather than just over a traveling show.

He enjoyed the backstage work, loved the way a disparate group of people could collaborate to pull together a play. He might not be on stage himself, but Jem got a thrill when the actors and the audience connected. A part of him still wanted to be an actor.

"Are you even listening, Jem?" Kaitlyn asked with an indignant scowl. "You just barely got here, and we're already boring you to death?"

"You're hardly boring me to death." He pushed back a little from the table and stretched out his legs, clasping his hands behind his head. "I was just focusing on this amazing food. That's the best food I've eaten since I was last home." Kaitlyn and his parents watched him expectantly, and he remembered that he had zoned out for a few seconds. He straightened and rested his elbows on the table. "So, while I was stuffing myself, what did I miss?"

"I'm going to England *next week*." Kaitlyn practically squealed as she said the last two words. "I just wish it was possible to go back in time and actually experience Regency England. But we'll come as close as we can. We already have a list of places we want to visit, so it'll be as close as we can get while still being in the 21st century."

"We?" Jem asked.

"Reese is coming too." His sister shot him a knowing look.

Jem's pulse sped up, both at the mention of Reese's name and at the way his sister was watching him. He hadn't thought she knew about his feelings for her friend. That had been part of why he'd left and not made an effort to contact Reese again. She'd begun to take over all his thoughts.

His sister and Reese had been best friends since junior high. The thought of trying to break into that group had stopped him dead. If things didn't work out between him and Reese, then what? And that had been assuming she would have been the least bit interested in him.

Too often over the last two years, especially when he was missing his family, Jem had regretted the decision not to push his luck and take a chance with Reese. Especially after that kiss.

"And don't forget Cora," Mother said.

"Who's Cora?" Jem asked.

"A new roommate." His mother rose from the table. "I understand how excited you all are to go on this trip, Kaitlyn, but I've seen those *Taken* movies, you know. I just worry about three young women going off to England with only one man to watch out for them."

"*One* man?" Jem asked. "Who's going?"

"Cyrus," Kaitlyn said. "He wants to check out the architecture."

Another friend from their childhood. The trip was sounding even better.

"How long are you going to be gone?" Jem asked.

"Four weeks. Would you like to come? You could room with Cyrus," Kaitlyn said, even more excited. "Do you still have your passport?"

"It should be in the boxes in the garage with the rest of my things." Jem's heart jumped at the possibilities, the important one being a chance to spend time with Reese again. He looked at his dad. "You guys didn't throw away my stuff, did you?"

"Of course not. We've always hoped you'd come home," his father said. "It would make your mother feel a lot better about this trip if you went along with them."

"It'll fit perfectly with my goals." Jem got to his feet with a grin. "I've always wanted a chance to work on my English accent."

"Your accent. *Right*." Kaitlyn shot him a knowing smirk.

"Yes. My accent." He kept his tone neutral, hoping the heat on his face didn't show.

"Oh, Jem." His mother threw her arms around him. "Thank you so much. I can sleep now, knowing the girls will be safe in your hands."

"They'd be safe with Cyrus," he said. "And if I have to renew my passport, I'll only be there for part of the time."

"I know." His mother shot him a look similar to Kaitlyn's, and he was struck by how much alike they were.

THE KICKBOXING VIDEO ENDED. Breathing heavily, Reese bent over to pick up her towel. She wiped her face and grabbed the water bottle on the floor. She hoped she'd be able to get in some exercise while they were traveling.

This trip to England both excited her and made her nervous.

She'd never had an opportunity to travel outside of the US before, and every couple of days, she'd pull out her shiny new passport, almost as though she needed to see it to believe she really had one. Even the tickets they had purchased together didn't seem as real as that passport did.

Her phone chimed with Kaitlyn's ring. Reese flung the hand towel over her shoulder and picked up her cell.

"Hey," she said.

"You know how freaked out my mom's been about us going on this trip, right?" Kaitlyn asked without any other intro.

"Yeah. Is she giving you a hard time about it again?" Reese asked.

"No. She's perfectly happy now."

"Okay." Something in Kaitlyn's voice made Reese pause. "What's changed?"

"Jem!"

"Um . . ." Reese's words died out. "Like your brother?"

"Of course, my brother. Seriously, how many guys do you know named Jem?"

"But, what does he have to do with our trip to London?"

"His tour finished, and he showed up this evening. He's coming with us. Isn't that awesome?" Kaitlyn's words came out faster. "I've missed him so much, and when we started talking about it, Mom went off on her sob story."

"Did your mother invite him along?" Reese asked, unsure. She had once thought herself in love with him, but that was ancient history. Then how come her heart was beating so quickly?

Jem, the buddy that she and his sister played with growing up. Being a couple of years older, he had turned into the cool one who'd run with so many different social groups. She'd felt like she had stayed the gawky Amazonian friend of his kid sister. All those years, in spite of her crush on him, Jem had never shown any signs that he thought of her in any other way than platonic, until the evening before he'd left on the Broadway tour.

She cast that memory aside. Two years could change people a lot, especially when one of them had been traveling around with a bunch of Broadway-level actors. And it wasn't like he'd made any effort to contact her. The kiss had meant nothing to him. It should mean nothing to her.

"No, Mom didn't invite him," Kaitlyn said. "*I* did. He seemed really interested when he found out about the trip, so I asked if he'd like to come along."

"And he said yes." Reese didn't know how she felt about his inclusion. "Does he even have a passport?"

"He does, but it's expired," Kaitlyn said. "He's going to pay to expedite it and should get it in two to three weeks."

"All right then." Reese knew it was too late to throw a fit now if he had already agreed to come. It would be a plus not to have to worry about Kaitlyn's mother nagging her all the time.

"I'm hoping he'll get there in time for the Regency Ball, but it might not be until after," Kaitlyn said.

"The ball," Reese said flatly. She had agreed to go along with the week-long Regency immersion experience, but she wasn't thrilled about the dancing. Unless it was exercise-related like Zumba, she had never been into dancing. Besides, her height never made her a desirable partner. A Regency ball. Her stomach dropped as a thought occurred to her. "Were you able to order me something to wear?"

"I checked. Our clothing comes as part of the package," Kaitlyn said. "They'll fit us once we're there. The hostess—she said everyone should call her Aunt Nellie—will have period gowns for us, and she'll provide lessons on how to dance and act and everything. This will be *so* much fun. Hey, I have to go. Talk to you later."

Reese cringed internally and wiped her face with the towel. She hadn't been looking forward to this part of the trip anyway, but now Jem was going to be there. The ball would be the perfect place for the too-tall American to make a total fool of herself.

In front of Jem.

Reese Hamilton has big plans to help make the world a better place. Then fae magic rips her back to 1850. She finds she must make a choice between two men and two times.

CHAPTER 1: FOR THE MAGIC

PRESENT DAY

"I want that place to burn, boy."

Michael Addington stared at his grandfather sitting in the overstuffed chair. With the death of Michael's father two months ago, he'd thought the old man's obsession with Twickenham Manor might finally wane, but he should have known better. That place had been a curse on his family, if only because the two men had refused to let go of their grudge. George Addington was nothing if not consistent.

"That's arson, Granddad." Michael kept his voice calm and soothing. "It's against the law."

"There's a higher law. *Thou shalt not suffer a witch to live.*"

Michael rubbed his temple against the headache building there. He was sick of that old biblical quote. His father and grandfather had fed it to Michael all through his youth. He'd even believed it until he'd gone to university. That was when he'd discovered for himself there were other translations and interpretations of that particular verse from Exodus.

"You've been saying that for twenty-five years, but you and Dad never did anything about it before. Why is this now my problem?"

"Don't you use that tone with me." The old man's face went red, and he leaned forward.

"No, don't. Please," Michael said gently. His father's sudden death had been hard on both of them, but especially on his grandfather. The two men had been best friends as well as father and son.

"They killed Harry." His grandfather clutched Michael's arm.

An unexpected chill ran down his spine. Could there really be a secret at Twickenham Manor? Could his grandfather be right? Had the two men discovered something the people at Twickenham wanted to hide?

Michael took a deep breath and reminded himself that having been raised by two conspiracy theorists made it too easy for him to be sucked into their nonsense. His grandfather's claim was ridiculous.

"Dad had a heart attack. That's what the doctor said."

"They do things over there with potions. That woman they call Aunt Nellie is a sorceress. Get up at dawn and watch her from the tower. What is it she gathers each morning? She uses it to make those cursed portraits."

Michael pinched the bridge of his nose. His grandfather had a powerful intensity about him, not a manic, crazed kind but one of conviction and sincerity.

"You've never told me how you know this."

The old man closed his eyes, his grip loosening on Michael's arm.

"That witch trapped me in her web, years ago." His grandfather's voice softened further. "That was when I met your grandmother."

Michael blinked. It was the first time he could remember his grandfather actually referring to her. Any reference to his grandmother had always been forbidden. She'd left when Michael's father had been six. George had passed on his bitterness of her abandonment of their family to his son. The two men had conspired for years on how to get even with the people at Twickenham whom, they claimed, had something to do with her leaving.

Or was it her disappearance? The hair on Michael's arms stood on end. Could the two men have been right all these years? Were there nefarious things happening at the manor? But how could it be? Aunt Nellie held week-long Regency immersion vacations and a monthly full-moon ball. If people were disappearing from the place, someone would have reported it. Wouldn't they?

"Witches," his grandfather whispered.

Michael met the old man's steely gaze. George might be old and emotionally broken from his decades of grief, but his mind was still sharp.

"I know what I'm talking about, boy. They have their little tonics and teas that change the way you feel; shift the way you think. They twist your mind and make you believe there's nothing wrong with what they do. And you believe them. You go along with it. It's sorcery, I tell you, and Aunt Nellie is a predator. She took my sweet—" His grandfather's voice broke.

Compassion swelled in Michael, and he took the old man's hand. He'd always been sour and curmudgeonly, and there were many times Michael had thought his grandmother had left because she couldn't take it anymore. That didn't however explain why she'd left her only child behind.

Michael had found a trunk upstairs in the old house once, filled with clothing and a few knickknacks. He'd never asked for confirmation, because his grandmother was a taboo subject, but he knew they were hers. There was a single photo that had made him wonder how a woman who'd smiled so lovingly at her husband and son could have abandoned them without looking back.

Reminding himself to take his grandfather's accusations with a grain of salt, Michael couldn't quite shake off his upbringing. Maybe he should look through the trunk again that was in the tower. There could be some hint of what had happened. It wouldn't hurt to go up at first light too. One of the windows overlooked the Twickenham grounds.

When he'd been a child, he'd enjoyed watching guests stroll the grounds in their period clothing. He tried to remember if he'd ever seen Aunt Nellie wandering the grounds at daybreak, but he couldn't recall a time when he'd been up there that early. Did she really go out every day to collect something? If so, what? After George's claim that they'd killed Michael's father, he'd have to find out.

"It's the portraits on the top floor," the old man said, his voice rough. "If we destroy them, it will end."

His grandfather's claims unsettled Michael more than he cared to admit. Surely, there had to be more to what was going on at Twickenham.

"I'll see what I can find out," he said.

1851

The Season that Ellen Hildebrand had anticipated for years had been a disappointment. Not a failure, certainly, as she had received four marriage proposals. She disliked the need to become proficient at letting men down, for she understood too well the pain of caring for someone who did not return the same feelings.

But she must not think of that. Over the past year, she had come to understand that she had been more in love with the idea of the man than in the man himself. And he had, after all, married her dearest friend. It had served as a good lesson for Ellen, one she had considered during her Season.

She picked up the ribbons she'd purchased for Catherine. Her sister-in-law was likely in the morning room. Grandmama had been teaching Catherine how to sew the sweetest tiny clothes. She and Gareth were hoping it was a boy. He needed an heir, after all. But Ellen wished it would be a little girl.

"We can't wait an extra month. We have to go tomorrow."

At the worry in Catherine's voice, Ellen paused outside the open door.

"But, my love, how will we explain returning so soon with a babe?"

Gareth's voice was the one he used when trying to sound soothing, but he always was unable to cover his own alarm, and it made the hair on Ellen's neck stand on end.

"We know too well how ill it makes us to travel," her brother continued, "what would it do to the baby?"

"A child born of parents from two times should not be greatly troubled by the travel," came the voice of Aunt Nellie from Twickenham Manor.

Ellen hadn't realized the woman had come to Kellworth. Then her words struck Ellen, and she rubbed her temples. Two times? What could that possibly mean?

"I need a decent stethoscope." The frustration in Catherine's voice pulled Ellen from her thoughts. "These last few weeks, I've gotten big, much bigger than I was last time. With the stethoscope, I'd know if I could hear two heartbeats."

"Twins?" Gareth asked, his voice strained, the fear powerful.

Ellen gave a soft gasp. *No. No.* She clenched her hands, crushing the carefully ironed ribbons. She found it hard to swallow. Losing his first wife in childbirth more than a decade ago had nearly destroyed him. How could he cope if he lost Catherine the same way?

"There's a greater risk of complications with twins, both for me and them. We need to travel soon."

How could Catherine wish to travel again so soon? They had barely returned to Kellworth, and the five-hour ride from London had made her poor ankles swell dreadfully. And where might she go?

"I fear, my love, that you are correct. We still have not settled on a way to break the news to Ellen and Grandmama that they may not be with you at your time," Gareth said. "You know they both expect it."

Ellen's heart sank. Was she not to be allowed to assist with the birth? Not assist, of course, but she had thought to be there to offer encouragement. Did Catherine not trust her?

Her brother said something, his voice tender but so soft Ellen couldn't make out his words. Which was probably for the best. Since marrying Catherine, Gareth was a changed man and embarrassingly happy. It was something she would not have imagined possible a year ago.

"I believe Catherine is correct that she should travel now, especially if there is a possibility she carries twins," Aunt Nellie said. "I suggest that you tell everyone you're going to rusticate at one of his lordships more rural estates. Your valet and her maid will have ruffled feathers, but that would be an issue anyway. You can tell them it is a good time for them to visit family, and that you plan to return in three months' time. You, of course, may remain longer, but you should return here with your healthy baby." The older woman gave a soft laugh. "Or *babies*."

Ellen closed her eyes and leaned against the wall. There was that reference to time again. How could Catherine's time be different than Gareth's? It made no sense.

"Yes." Catherine's voice sounded relieved now. "That's exactly what we'll do. You know, I've had the oddest feelings lately. It's probably just pregnancy hormones, but it's making me edgy."

"You, as well, my love?" Gareth asked.

"Yes."

"I, as well," Aunt Nellie said, a note of worry in her voice now that Ellen had never heard before. "The magic has been warning me of pending danger."

Magic? Ellen shook her head. She must have misheard, so she leaned closer to the door.

"What kind of danger?" Gareth asked, his tone now firm and businesslike. "Does it have anything to do with Catherine?"

"No," Aunt Nellie said thoughtfully. "But it does have something to do with your family."

"Ellen?" Catherine asked.

"Perhaps. Perhaps not. But we must all be on guard. My dear, your tea has gotten cold. Let me pour you another cup."

An odd dizziness made Ellen feel as though she might fall. She closed her eyes. Was she feverish and had not heard right? No. She had not imagined it; she was sure. What was she to make of all this talk of magic and different times? To hear her ever-practical brother accept such statements as though they were commonplace was the stuff of dreams.

Had Ellen not come down the stairs but fallen asleep in her chair and was dreaming? It was all so strange. Since returning to Kellworth, she'd had an odd sense of expectancy. If Ellen had to put a word to the feeling, she'd have named it a premonition. But she would not use the word and certainly not in front of Grandmama. Her spinster great aunt claimed that some members of the family had the "sight," which was stuff and nonsense. The elderly woman had often had similar flights of fancy, and Ellen had suggested she should have been an authoress.

Adding to Ellen's sense of unease was all the talk of magic, different times, and traveling somewhere to have the baby without any of the family in attendance.

"Are you not well, my Lady?"

At the voice of her brother's valet, Ellen startled and opened her eyes. Her cheeks went warm, and she had to struggle to keep her composure.

"No, Thomas. I'm fine. I was simply looking for Lady Catherine."

"I imagine they are in her ladyship's morning room." He indicated the open doorway.

Ellen narrowed her eyes at the older man. His face held the mellow expression it always did, but she was sure there was a hint of humor in his voice. Though, considering what she thought she'd just heard, she might be imagining that as well.

"I thought I might have heard Aunt Nellie's voice and did not wish to disturb them." Not that she had need to make excuses to one of the servants. If she wished to lean against a wall, Ellen was certainly within her rights to do so.

"As you say, my Lady."

"Ellen, is that you?" Gareth appeared in the doorway. "And Thomas is here. Good. You both should know that her ladyship and I have decided to visit Ravensdon House for a lengthy visit until after the baby is born. We're leaving straightaway. Thomas, I'll need you to pack. And . . . I will not be needing your services so you will have time to visit your sister."

"But, my Lord—"

"No." Gareth held up his hand, his tone firm. "It's been decided. We will leave tomorrow. Please inform Alice, so she may begin packing for her ladyship. She will also be able to visit her family."

Thomas didn't argue further but gave a crisp bow and walked away.

"My dear, Ellen," Gareth said, putting a hand on her shoulder, "I know you've been looking forward to being there to assist Catherine, but I'm afraid the doctor has suggested that just she and I go. I *am* sorry."

He lied so glibly. She had meant to argue with him about leaving her behind, but the way his shoulders appeared to carry the weight of the world, she couldn't. Not since he had come out of his doldrums had she seen him look so burdened. In the other room, Aunt Nellie was saying something to Catherine, and an idea came to Ellen.

"Gareth," she said, putting a hand on his arm, "do you think

Aunt Nellie would allow me to stay with her while you're gone? With Grandmama visiting her old friends in Bath, I don't wish to stay here alone. I would require a companion. That would take time, and you are in a rush."

"That is a brilliant idea." He looked at her, his eyes full of affection and relief. "It would take a great deal off my mind if I knew you were in a comfortable situation, and I know you enjoy visiting Twickenham. Will you come and have tea with us? Aunt Nellie is here, and we can inquire about your stay."

"Of course."

"What are you holding?" He indicated her clenched fist, colorful ribbons leaking between her fingers.

"Oh, it's nothing that won't wait." Ellen slid them into her pocket and followed her brother into the morning room.

When Lady Ellen Hildebrand is ripped to the future, she finds herself not only fighting for the fae magic that sent her but also for her life.

Get *For the Magic* on Amazon.

ABOUT THE AUTHOR

Award-winning author, wife, mother, grandmother, Harry Potter geek, Army veteran, karate black belt, and online gamer.

BOOKS BY DONNA K. WEAVER

The *Safe Harbors* Series

A Change of Plans (#1)

Hope's Watch (#1.5)

Torn Canvas (#2)

A Season of Change (#2.5)

Swing Vote (#3)

Kings Crossed Lovers (#4)

***Ripple Effect Romance Novella (#5)* Series**

Second Chances 101

Solo Titles

Teapots & Treachery

***Twickenham Full-Moon Ball Romances* Series**

Against the Magic

With the Magic

For the Magic

***Billionaires of REKD* Series**

Hiding with the Billionaire (#1)

Luck of the Billionaire (#2)

Three Fortunes for the Billionaire (#3)

A Lass for the Billionaire (#4)

The *Gift* Series

The Gift of a Child

The Forever Gift

***Lilac City Romance Novella* Series**

A Match for Maude

A Dandy for Doris

A Lady for Luke (coming)

A Fella for Frances

ACKNOWLEDGMENTS

No book is ever written alone, even though it might seem that way as I sit in my office writing away. My wonderful husband Edward is the best support any author could as for.

My critique partners are wonderful as always. I'd like to thank Canda, Alison, and Meredith for taking to time to read and offer feedback. I really appreciate the guidance or my editor Katharina Brendel.

COPYRIGHT

With the Magic

Edited by Katharina Brendel, Portable Magic Editing Services

Cover design by Bret Henderson Design

Author photo by Sherry Ward of SW Portraits

ISBN eBook: 978-1-946152-17-6

ISBN Paperback: 978-1-946152-18-3

ISBN Audiobook: 978-1-946152-19-0

Printed in the United States of America

Donna K. Weaver's author website is www.donnakweaver.com.

CPSIA information can be obtained
at www.ICGtesting.com
Printed in the USA
FSHW020648010220
66690FS